It was pitch black down there. When I flipped the light switch at the top of the stairs, it didn't work. "Dad, it's me." I listened, but I couldn't hear anything. "Dad, are you down there?"

I found the rail and reached for the next step down with my foot. "Dad?"

Nothing again. I couldn't even hear Dad's breathing. Why would he be so quiet? I finally got all the way down to the bottom and felt the cement under my feet. In one corner, I could see the pale gleam of the freezer. Across the room, there was the washer and dryer.

Where was Dad? I saw another light above and pulled the string. This time, the light flashed on. It cast a dim glow over everything. Then I spotted him.

He was over in the far corner of the basement, his back to me. He was working on something in the light of a small utility lamp. I hurried toward him, my shoes quiet on the concrete. "Dad?" My voice seemed to lack any volume and it was almost shaking.

"You forgot Max's food." I forced myself to speak up, and the effect was awful. Dad must have jumped a foot before he spun around. In one hand he held a pistol. And it was pointed right at me!

Daddy, Please Tell Me What's Wrong

by Shannon Kennedy

Cover photo by John Strange

Published by Willowisp Press, Inc.
401 E. Wilson Bridge Road, Worthington, Ohio 43085

Copyright © 1988 by Willowisp Press, Inc.

Printed in the United States of America
10 9 8 7 6 5 4 3 2 1

ISBN 0-87406-239-X

One

WE were supposed to be writing essays about the Civil War, but my brain was on hold. I just couldn't forget the way that my dad had hollered about my messy bedroom before I left for school. Normally, that kind of stuff just rolls off my shoulders.

If Mom were home, she'd say to cut my dad some slack. Dad's temper has been getting worse and worse since he lost his job almost a year ago. And the fact that Mom was working in California for the Army Reserve and wouldn't be back in Washington State before the end of the month didn't help matters.

Every year Mom goes away for two weeks of active-duty training, and we all manage to get along without her. But this time Mom had been asked to stay on for a few more weeks. We needed her paycheck, so she had to accept the offer.

I stared at the blank sheet of paper in front of me and then at the chalkboard again. *Take it easy, Jennifer Conway*, I told myself. *Dad gets mad quickly but he'll be over it by the time you get home*.

The Civil War? What did I remember about it from all of Mr. Brown's lectures? Not much. I just couldn't focus on dates and battles. Instead, I kept wondering what the people who fought were like. They were young, I knew that. How did they feel about leaving their families and going off to war?

Mr. Brown sat at his desk in the front of the room, grading papers. I couldn't talk to him about it. When I had brought up things like this before, he had just sighed and shaken his head. He was already irked because I'd been late this morning.

But it wasn't my fault. My alarm clock hadn't gone off this morning. And Tim, my 11-year-old brother, counts on me to get him up—so he'd been late, too. I had to pound on his door twice. Dad had been working on one of his special projects down in the basement. He'd stayed up all night again, and he always forgets about time these days.

Mr. Brown looked up and saw me staring. I tried to pretend to start writing, but he stood up and came toward my desk. He's young, barely out of college and sometimes he tries to be buddy-buddy with students. It seems sort of phony, but I like him anyway.

"What's the matter, Jenny?"

"Nothing," I answered.

Mr. Brown sighed and rubbed his forehead. "You're one of my best students, Jenny. If there's a problem, I'd like to know about it. Is the test too hard?"

"No, sir." I often call men "sir." I think it's because Dad makes us call him "sir." He's strict about what he calls "good manners."

"I was thinking about the actual people who fought in the Civil War, not about the battles or the leaders, but the men themselves." I stopped as another thought came to me. "And what about the women? Did women go to war back then like they do now?"

Mr. Brown's entire face took on a frown. "That's not part of the test, Jennifer. Now, just concentrate on your essay and answer one of the questions. Try number three. It's about the Gettysburg Address."

I picked up my pen and figured I could fake it. I started writing.

"That's better," Mr. Brown said approvingly and started away.

I decided that I'd ask Dad about whether women fought in the Civil War. He liked to give me answers and get me thinking. He said I had a good mind, and it was a shame the school didn't tap it. Dad's like that. He doesn't always respect authority, but he does know all about wars and military history.

*　*　*　*　*　*

It was cold that afternoon during phys ed. There was a breeze off Port Gardner Bay. As we waited at the track for class to start, I shivered in my shorts and T-shirt, wishing I'd brought my sweats. Miss Robbins blew her whistle. Finally we were going to get started.

"All right, girls. Let's do two laps around the track and warm up."

While almost everybody else stood around, not wanting to begin, I did a few stretching exercises. I noticed that my best friend, Bonnie Williams, was stretching, too, and I grinned at her. She smiled back at me, and I took off around the track. It was the only way to get warm.

Bonnie caught up with me in a few moments. "What did you think of that history test this morning? Wasn't it awful?"

"Yeah. And I made the mistake of asking Mr. Brown if women went to war. He wasn't too pleased with that!"

"He can be a jerk sometimes," Bonnie puffed, pushing at her golden blond hair. "Are you going to slow down?"

"I missed my three miles this morning. I want to make up for it now."

Bonnie dropped back. "Go ahead. I know my limits."

I laughed. "See you later." If Bonnie had an older brother like mine, she'd have learned to run at an early age. Richard and I had played together a lot as kids, but now it seemed we just argued all the time. Ever since Richard turned 16, he's fought with everyone, especially Dad. Maybe it was Richard's fault that Dad has been so tense lately.

Poor Dad. He had this dream of one of his kids joining the Marines. But Richard is hooked on computers. He plans to be a programmer. He runs in marathons on weekends unless he's competing in a karate tournament. Richard never had much interest in the military. He never played soldier when he was younger like I did.

As for my younger brother, he was a bookworm. Tim learned to read when he was four, and his nose has been stuck in a book ever since. Sometimes I feel sorry for the authors of the books he reads. Tim always tries out the stuff that's in the story, and if it doesn't work, he writes letters to the writers and tells them so. Sometimes, the authors even write back.

It must be hard for Dad, knowing his boys are not military types. My brothers look just like him, though. They both have sandy hair and dark brown eyes. I have green eyes like Mom, but she always says I'm more like my dad than anybody else in the family. So I'm obviously the one who's going to enlist in the Marines as soon as I'm old enough. I don't mind. I like being outdoors and I love visiting military installations. Dad takes me to the museums, and we watch the troops drilling whenever we can.

Dad was still in the Marines when I was a little kid, and I learned how to count by listening to the sergeants call out numbers as they marched the soldiers around the base. Dad used to sing a few of the marching songs when he was working around the yard, but lately he hasn't been singing much.

I ran past two older boys and noticed that they weren't from the junior high. That meant the high school classes were out here, too, and I wondered what Miss Robbins was thinking. Usually, she tries to keep us separate from the older guys. I shoved at my shoulder-length, dark hair and wished I'd bothered to tie the curls back. Well, it was too late now.

I heard someone pounding behind me and risked a quick look over my shoulder in case Bonnie had decided to take the exercise seriously. It was some boy, not Bonnie. He was nice-looking, even with his dark hair clinging wetly to his tanned forehead.

He came up beside me and ran even with me. "You're fast," he said.

"So are you." I kept on at my regular pace.

"I've already done my laps," the boy remarked. "I don't know how long I can stay with you."

I kept going. "Quit if you want. I'm just getting started."

When I finished my second lap, he was still with me. I saw some of the other girls from my class. They were finally starting to run slowly around the track. I began another lap.

"How far are you going?" the boy asked, puffing.

"I usually do five miles a day. Three in the morning and two at night. I'll just go till the other girls get done. What about you? How far do you run?"

"I'd done three miles before I caught up with you. If you weren't here, I'd quit."

I tried to ignore the way my stomach bounced at the compliment. "Go ahead. I'm not stopping you." I spotted Miss Robbins talking to another teacher and she waved me over. I slowed down and jogged to her. "You wanted me?"

"How many laps have you done, Jenny?"

"Almost three. I'm trying to get in my usual five miles."

Miss Robbins smiled and touched my shoulder. "First, let me introduce you to the track coach. This is Mr. Fisher. He's really impressed with you. Drake Stevens is our best cross-country runner, and you didn't have any trouble at all keeping up with him."

"I'd have made her work harder," the dark-haired boy said as he came up beside me, "but I'd already done my miles."

Mr. Fisher grinned at us. He seemed nice and a typical outdoorsman, tanned and fit. "How about joining the junior high team, Jenny? We can always use strong runners."

I shook my head. "No, thanks. I'm supposed to watch my little brother in the afternoons while my mom's out of town. And I have chores and stuff to do every day, too."

Mr. Fisher raked a hand through his graying hair and gave me a look almost like one of Dad's. "What if I talk to your folks?"

I shrugged. "Go ahead, but my dad doesn't like school sports. He won't let me." I knew I should have showed more interest, but joining the track team just didn't seem possible. With going to the rifle range on weekends, karate classes after school, and studying military tactics with my dad, it was all I could do to manage time to be with Bonnie. Even if a little part of me wanted to be on the team, I didn't know how I'd find time. "Can I finish my miles now?"

Miss Robbins looked at me questioningly. "Jenny, I wish you'd give this some more thought. Joining the track team could be good training for you—didn't you tell me once you want to enlist in the Marines when you graduate from high school? The physical training and the team spirit would—"

"I thought the Marines were only looking for a few good men," Drake interrupted teasingly.

I looked Drake up and down. "Then you don't have anything to worry about." I trotted back toward the track. By talking about my plans, Miss Robbins had made me feel like a fool in front of Drake and the coach. I was 13, not a little girl, and my plan to join the Marines was not just a childish dream. I started running again, and Bonnie caught up with me after a few strides.

"What did he say?" Bonnie demanded. "What? What?" Bonnie was full of oxygen. If she hadn't been running, she would have been jumping up and down in excitement.

"Who?" I asked, although I knew she was interested in my conversation with Drake. "Mr. Fisher? He wants me on the track team."

"Who cares about that old fogy?" Bonnie grabbed my arm. "I mean Drake Stevens. He's such a . . ." She sighed dreamily.

"Jerk," I finished for her.

"Jenny, no!" Bonnie wailed. "You didn't! Tell me you didn't put down the best athlete in the entire school."

"I always knew Cedar Hills was small, but is *he* the best we can do?" I snapped.

"I knew it. You were rude to him. How could you, Jennifer Conway?"

"I wasn't rude," I replied hotly.

"I'll bet," Bonnie glared, blue eyes hard. "What did you say? I'll bet it was something nasty."

"I was sugary-sweet, sickeningly sweet, and I didn't say anything I'm ashamed of." I often wonder why Bonnie is so hung up on boys. Maybe it's because her folks are getting a divorce and she wants the security of having a boyfriend. She doesn't have any brothers or sisters. There are two boys in my family, and I know what the male gender is *really* like.

They don't wash dishes, do laundry, mow the lawn, pick up their socks, or feed Max the

14

dog. The only time those two brothers of mine do their work is when Mom's home or Dad's on the warpath.

I was pretty certain that most guys are the same. Professional athletes don't do laundry commercials, they do shaving cream ads. Housework isn't macho, so I'd bet Drake Stevens doesn't do it either. He probably has his mom or a maid to take care of him.

"I don't know what's wrong with you, Jennifer Conway. You don't like any boys, do you?" Bonnie puffed.

"I love my dad."

"Jenny!" Bonnie exploded and tried to catch her breath. "We aren't talking about dads. We're talking about boys. Will you keep your brain on the conversation?"

I slowed way down but I kept running. Bonnie's face was getting bright red, and I knew she must be getting tired.

"Look, Bonnie. I liked Drake Stevens fine until he started teasing me for wanting to be a Marine," I told her.

Bonnie sniffed. "So, he's a chauvinist. But he *is* cute."

I shook my head and waved her away as we circled past the spot where Miss Robbins and Mr. Fisher had been standing. I started to wish I could take Mr. Fisher up on the invitation to join the track team. But at the moment, my life was just too complicated.

* * * * *

Our house was dark that afternoon when I walked in. The living-room curtains were still closed. I put my books on the coffee table and went to the windows to open the drapes, letting the sunlight in.

"What are you doing?" Dad said loudly, and I must have jumped 10 feet.

I turned around and saw him sitting in his armchair in the corner of the room. He's been doing that a lot lately—just sitting quietly by himself. "I just wanted to let in some light."

"If I had wanted the drapes open, I would have opened them!" There was anger in Dad's voice, but I pretended not to notice it. What kind of Marine would I make if I acted scared of my own father? I jerked the drapes closed and grabbed my books. "Then sit in the dark. See if I care."

Dad reached for the lamp on the table beside him and switched it on. "Are you trying to make me lose my temper, young lady?"

I shook my head, eyeing him with some concern. His sandy hair was short by most people's standards, but it was still too long for him, and he hadn't shaved today. I was pretty sure he'd worn that pair of jeans yesterday. What was the matter with him? "Are you okay, Dad?"

"I'm fine," Dad barked. "Or I would be if you and your brothers would help out once in a while. This house is a mess!"

He was right—the place really was a mess. I hurried across to his chair and hugged him. "I'll clean it up. I'm sorry I was so rude."

Dad sat like a statue for a second before he hugged me back. "Thanks, honey. I don't mean to nag you so much. I guess I'm just worried about your mom."

"She's fine," I promised and kissed his cheek. "And she'll be home before we know it."

Dinner was pretty peaceful that night. Richard made a salad for once, and he didn't complain about Dad's spaghetti even though the sauce was a little scorched. Tim and I were in the middle of washing the dishes when the phone rang. It was Mom.

While my brothers talked to her, I went into the living room to get Dad. He was back in his chair again, but this time he was staring at the television. There was only one problem—the TV wasn't on. Whatever pictures Dad was looking at were only in his mind.

Two

THAT episode stayed on my mind for the rest of the evening and throughout the next morning. Mr. Brown got mad at me for not paying attention in class, but how could I listen to a history lecture? I was really worried about Dad. He just wasn't himself lately.

Should I tell Mom about it? How could I? She was counting on all of us to be okay while she was working. She expected us to be what she called "system support." She couldn't take care of us and be a soldier at the same time.

I thought of going to talk to Richard about it, but he was over at the high school, three blocks away. I'd get suspended if I was caught leaving the junior high campus. Then Dad would *really* have a reason to be angry.

But talking to Richard at home was impossible. If he wasn't working on some new computer program, he and Dad were arguing.

Besides, Tim occasionally overhears private conversations and repeats them at the worst time. The last thing I needed was to have Dad know about my worries.

The only solution was to go see Richard at school, and hope we could talk. If I went at lunchtime, no one would miss me. I'd be careful and nobody would know. The decision made me feel better. I could actually listen to Mr. Brown talk about our class reports.

"I'm going to assign partners and you'll work together to present a report on the country you're given."

I crossed my fingers under the desk, hoping for a good partner. If only Bonnie had history the same period I did! We would be able to write a great report together.

My luck was the worst. I ended up with Diana, one of the biggest snobs in the entire school. She looked across the room at me and sniffed. I gave her a look of my own and then focused my attention back on Mr. Brown. He was assigning the countries now.

Diana raised her hand. "Can we ask for a country?"

Mr. Brown nodded and smiled at her. "Of course. If your partner agrees, you can do your report on almost any country you choose."

"Then I want to do Vietnam."

There was silence while Mr. Brown looked at me. Most of the kids know my mom is in the Reserve and that my dad has a military background, too. I leaned back in my chair and pretended to examine my pencil. "No."

"What did you say, Jenny?" Mr. Brown asked in a stern voice.

I met his gaze. "I said no. I don't want to do a report on Vietnam or any country near it."

"Well, *I* should get a say in what the report's about," Diana protested, "as long as I have to have *her* for a partner."

For once I wished my karate master would let us punch people out. But *Sensei* Larkin is very strict, and his first rule is that we can't use karate unless we're in real trouble. While I might enjoy socking Diana one, it wasn't worth being demoted in front of my karate class. I started toward Mr. Brown's desk.

"But both partners have to agree," I said. "And I don't care what Diana says about me, I won't do a report on Vietnam."

I could have sworn there was a faint twinkle in Mr. Brown's eyes when he walked over to me and touched my shoulder.

"Sit down, Jenny. You don't have to work on Vietnam. Why don't the two of you report on Mexico?" Diana began to complain, but Mr. Brown held up his hand for quiet. "Diana, you can't call the shots alone on this. Obviously, Jenny has strong feelings about the subject, and I want to be fair to both of you. I'm assigning Mexico to you two."

I really had to respect Mr. Brown for taking such a firm stand. It isn't always easy to manage stubborn kids, but he'd done a good job. "Thank you, sir," I said as I sat down.

After class was over, I went up to his desk. The room was emptying quickly. "My dad was in Vietnam. We don't talk about it at home," I explained.

Mr. Brown leaned back in his chair, his dark eyes sober. "It might help if you did discuss it," he offered. "How long was your dad there? A year?"

I shook my head. "That was the standard tour, but my dad was a Marine. Marines stayed for tours of thirteen months, and Dad was there twice."

"Well, you don't have to do a report on the subject." Mr. Brown rubbed his jaw. "Mexico should keep you busy. Do you think you and Diana will be able to work together?"

"I don't know, sir, but I'm willing to try." Mr. Brown grinned at me, and his smile didn't seem phony at all. I had a funny feeling that we might grow to like each other.

* * * * *

Bonnie was at our locker when I got there at noon. I stuffed my books inside and slammed the door. Phys ed was right after lunch, so I wouldn't need any books for the moment. "I'm going to the high school to see Richard."

Bonnie looked startled. "We're not allowed to leave campus. You know that. They'll kill you. And you can see your brother at home."

"Today's my karate class. I go straight there after school. I've got to see Richard now. Go to lunch without me."

Bonnie took a deep breath. "I'm coming with you. If we get caught, we'll tell them it's a family emergency."

"Are you sure you want to go? I don't want to get you in trouble with your mom, especially with the way you two are arguing."

Bonnie gave me a strange look. "I'm *always* in trouble with Mom. I don't think we'll ever get along again. And I don't care. So, let's go. Besides, your brother is gorgeous."

Bonnie and boys, I thought with a sigh. We hurried out the side door and across the baseball field. Some of the kids saw us but I knew they wouldn't snitch.

We found Richard—as I had predicted—in the computer lab. He wasn't alone. Working at the next terminal was, of all people, Drake Stevens. I heard Bonnie take a sharp breath, and it's a wonder she didn't faint. Even I was glad to see Drake, in spite of the crack he'd made the day before about the Marines.

Drake saw us before Richard did, and he gave me a friendly smile. I remembered my own snappy reply to his teasing, and I was glad he didn't seem to be bearing a grudge.

"Well, if it isn't the Lone Runner." Drake smiled. "Are you looking for me?"

I was grateful that I didn't blush. "No. I wanted to see my brother. Richard, we've got to talk."

Richard glared at me like he always does when he thinks I'm being a pest. "You're just trying to get me in trouble. You know you're not supposed to be here."

"Mellow out, Rich," Drake ordered. He stood up and turned off his computer. "We'll take them back to the junior high and nobody will know. I can keep my mouth shut."

I was glad Drake wanted to help, but I doubted that Richard would. Boys are funny that way, and Richard is even more stubborn than most guys. That's probably why he fights so much with Dad. Neither one of them will admit that he ever needs anyone's assistance.

"Yeah," Bonnie chirped. "And if you don't

hurry up, we *will* get caught."

I glared at her. "Give me a chance to talk to Richard, will you?" I turned to him. "Please, Richard. It's important."

Richard turned off his computer and got up. "All right," he agreed. He gave me a dirty look. "But I'm counting on you not to cause trouble. I'm sick of Dad blaming me for things you and Tim pull."

I didn't say anything. How could I? With Bonnie and Drake standing there, I wasn't going to make a big scene. I didn't think we should gripe about Dad in front of our friends, and I'd never known Richard to do it before now. He used to demand that Tim and I be very respectful when we talked about Mom and Dad. Why was he acting so crass now? Was he just showing off, playing tough?

For about the millionth time, I wished Mom were home. Sometimes I think mothers aren't supposed to be sergeants in the Army. They're supposed to stay home and bake cookies. That thought almost made me laugh out loud. My mom can never remember if there's something in the oven till it's burning. Dad used to tease her about that.

Bonnie and Drake were walking ahead of us so Richard and I could talk privately. He waited until we were a block away from his school. "What do you want?"

I scuffed my shoe against the pavement. There were two more blocks to the junior high. I'd have liked to have lit into Richard, but I didn't dare, not when I needed his help. "It's Dad. I'm worried about him. He's not sleeping. He watches TV till sign-off and then he goes to the basement."

"He's an adult," Richard retorted. "He can do whatever he likes. And you know he's never needed much sleep."

"What about the way he sits with his back to a wall?" I demanded. "A couple of days ago when Tim was sitting in his chair, Dad really freaked and dumped him on the floor. He never used to do things like that."

"Tim shouldn't have been sitting in Dad's chair," Richard said. "You know how Dad is about his territory. He guards it. Jenny, Dad's fine. Just stay out of his way. That's what I do."

I stuffed my hands in the pockets of my jeans and tried not to cry. "I'm scared about him. And I don't want to stay out of the way of my own father. I think we ought to call Mom."

"What?" Richard yelled. "You're nuts."

Drake turned to look at us and I tried to stay calm. I kept my voice low. "I just think she ought to know."

"Yeah," Richard snapped. "That's a really good idea. She'd leave the job and that would cause her grief with the Army. Jenny, she isn't working for a company where she can quit and walk out the door. Besides, we need the money. If we didn't, Mom wouldn't have stayed on for the extra duty. You have to grow up . . . and so does Dad."

We stood in the gate and I eyed Richard hopefully. He was my big brother. When I was younger, he had seemed to have all the answers. It seemed like he still should. A tear trickled down my cheek and I bit my lip hard.

Richard tugged on my hair. "He's okay, honest. But I'll watch him and see if he's acting weird. If he is, we'll call Mom. Right?"

"Right." I tried to smile and I wiped at my face. I wanted to believe Richard—I really did. But some inner warning kept flashing inside my head. There was something wrong with Dad. Only what was it? I just didn't know.

I started through the gate with Bonnie, and Drake gave me a steady look. I hoped he didn't know how upset I really was.

"Did you get the problem all worked out?" Drake asked. He wasn't smiling and his brown eyes were sober. "Or can I help?"

I shook my head. What would Drake say about the strange things Dad was doing?

Would he be like Richard and think Dad was normal? "Thanks for asking, but there isn't much anybody can do right now." I met Drake's gaze. "I'm sorry if I was rude yesterday."

Drake's slow smile warmed his entire face. "No problem. How about if we go running together tomorrow? At lunchtime?"

"No way," Richard ordered. "Dad'll go crazy. He thinks you're too young to date."

"Who said anything about dating?" Drake asked. "I said running. I have to work to keep up with Jenny.

"I have first lunch." I glanced at Drake again. "I'll meet you at the track."

"You do and I'll tell Dad," Richard threatened. "I'm not having him on my case about this, too."

"You won't have to say anything." I tossed my head. "Dad's picking me and Tim up tonight at the *dojo*. I'll ask him then. Come on, Bonnie, or we'll be late."

"If it makes him feel better, tell him that Bonnie will be there, too," Drake suggested. "You can run with us, can't you?"

"I'll die on the first lap," Bonnie laughed. "You'll have to drag me behind you."

Bonnie and I left Drake and Richard at the gate and headed for the main building. "I'm sorry about missing lunch," I said. "And Richard. Sometimes he's like a bear with a really bad toothache."

"That's all right," Bonnie offered. She paused and then said, "Jenny I don't understand all those karate words you've started using. What's a *dojo*?"

"The *dojo* is what we call the karate school in Japanese," I replied. "Since the technique comes from Japan, we're also supposed to be learning the language. I can count for exercises, say the creed, and name my *katas*."

"What's a *kata*?" Bonnie inquired.

"It's an imaginary fight with several opponents," I said. "You learn all the correct moves for each *kata*—they're like exercises. That's the way *Sensei* explains it. I know about 38 different *katas*. And, oh, yes—*Sensei* is the teacher at the *dojo*."

"Is he nice?" Bonnie asked.

I laughed. "Sometimes. Usually, Sensei Larkin is lots more strict than our teachers here. Like we have to remember to bow whenever he enters the room and if we forget, then we have to do knuckle push-ups. Once Tim was giving me a hard time at the *dojo*, and he had to do 50 of them."

"That's awesome," Bonnie grinned. "Talk about training brothers. Maybe your Sensei could do the same thing with Richard."

"That's not quite the way it works!" I told her. Now I had to explain about senior belts and treating the more advanced students with courtesy. "Richard's two stripes ahead of me. If I'm rude to him, I can lose my belt and be demoted. The same thing happens if we get into fights and hurt people with our karate."

"So much for the movies," Bonnie sighed. "I thought all karate experts got to beat people up."

"Only if we're in danger," I said. "If I thought Richard was really going to hit me, I could hit him back. But he'd be done for when Sensei got hold of him, not to mention Dad."

"Your dad sure is strict." Bonnie pulled open the door to the building. "But I like him."

"So do I." That was really true, and I eyed Bonnie. She was smart and could see below the surface. "Would you stay over on Friday? I know Dad'll agree if it's okay with your mom. I need your help."

* * * * *

Bonnie was pretty sure her mom would let her spend the night. She was going to check and call me later. We usually spent the night together at my house instead of hers, mostly because of my dollhouses. It's an incredible collection. Dad made me the first one when I was 10. Since then, I've gotten a new one for every birthday and every Christmas. I tried to tell Dad that I'm getting too old to play with dollhouses now. But recently I saw a picture of a castle that would make a fantastic addition to the collection. So I started hinting.

Dad had grumbled that one wall of my bedroom already looked like Main Street, U.S.A., but I reminded him that I still had an empty corner. He didn't say either yes or no regarding the castle. He just muttered something about it being a challenge.

I knew Dad wouldn't mind about Bonnie sleeping over on Friday. I'd ask him and make sure that the regular rules applied before she came. My folks have this theory about rules—they have to be able to trust us to figure out the rules in advance, and then to stick to them without a lot of nagging. The idea is that *we're* responsible for applying the rules. It works pretty well. That doesn't mean I don't make mistakes. I do, and so do my brothers. But we don't lie about them. That's one rule that's above all the others.

* * * * *

Karate on Wednesday is easy. All we have to do is warm up. Then we practice our blocks, punches, and kicks. After that we learn our new *kata*, or routine.

The *dojo* session that Wednesday ran late, but when we came out there was no sign of Dad. Usually, he'll sit in the car and read a book or the paper while he waits. Today he wasn't there.

Tim walked down to the corner to see if he was parked further away, but I didn't think he'd find him. For some reason, I knew Dad wasn't coming. Tim came back to stand beside me. Normally, he's pretty cocky. Right now, he looked scared. "Should we take the bus, Jenny?"

I shook my head and watched the downtown traffic whiz by. "Nope. By the time we get to the bus stop, Dad'll probably be here. He'll get worried and then be mad at us. You stay outside and watch for him. I'll use the phone inside to call home. He could be down in the basement. Maybe he just forgot to watch the time."

"Yeah," Tim cheered up a little. "He's really excited about your Christmas present."

I started to ask Tim about the castle, but then I changed my mind. I could pump Tim later. Right now, I needed to get us home. I glanced up and down the street one more time, but I didn't see our car anywhere. So I went back inside the karate school. Kicking off my shoes, I bowed to the teacher with the beginning class. Then I went across to the other door and did the ceremonial bow again before I entered the office.

Sensei Larkin was checking some papers and he asked me in Japanese what the problem was.

I paused, trying to think how to answer in Japanese. I've been working on my vocabulary, but I just hadn't learned the words for this situation. So I used English. "Dad was supposed to come pick us up, but he's not here. May I use the phone?"

"Of course. If something's wrong, I'll drive you home myself." Sensei Larkin moved so I could reach the receiver.

I dialed my number and waited while it rang almost forever. Finally, Richard answered.

"This is Jenny. Is Dad there? Did he forget that this is karate day?"

"He left ages ago," Richard said impatiently. "He'll be there soon. And by the way, I told him about you and Drake. He hit the roof. He said there was no way he'd let you go running with some high school boy."

Tears burned their way down my cheeks and lodged in my throat so I could barely breathe. "You stink, Richard. You really stink."

Three

WE waited at the *dojo* until nearly eight, but Dad didn't show up. Sensei Larkin drove us home. Dad wasn't at the house either. I was worried about him, but I didn't think he'd been in an accident or anything like that. I didn't know what was wrong, just that something was.

Tim went into Richard's room to show off his new *kata*, and I went straight upstairs. If I never saw my older brother again, it would be too soon. I thought about phoning Mom, but I knew she wouldn't get the message tonight unless I lied and said it was an emergency. I couldn't do that regardless of how much I wanted to talk to her.

I flopped on my bed and switched on the lamp. Looking across the room, I could see all my dollhouses, from the Victorian one to the southern plantation mansion. Next to those was a log cabin and then a ranch rambler. The fifth one was a brick colonial, followed by a condo and then a ski lodge.

There was a knock on my door, and I turned my head. "What?"

"Bonnie's on the phone," Tim called. "Do you want to talk to her or should I tell her to call back tomorrow?"

I got up. "You mean Richard's going to allow me to speak to my best friend? How generous of him!" I opened the door.

"If you two are fighting, keep me out of it," Tim said. He pushed at his sandy hair and scowled at me. "Richard's okay. Just stay off his back."

"Then he'd better get off mine and keep his nose out of my life," I retorted. I went in the kitchen and picked up the receiver. "Hi, Bonnie. What did your mom say?"

"It's fine with her," Bonnie reported. "She wants to go out with her new boyfriend, and I guess I cramp her style anyway."

"Well, Richard's cramping mine," I grumbled. "He told my dad I'm going running with Drake, and there's going to be big trouble around here."

"What a creep," Bonnie exclaimed. "And I happen to know that Drake's really looking forward to running with you. He's going to be really disappointed if your dad won't let you go."

"How do you know that?" I asked. "Or are you just guessing?"

"I talked to Drake on the way home from school today," Bonnie said, laughing. "I *thought* you'd be interested in this! You know, I think he really likes you. He thinks you're different."

"Me?" I gasped. "I'm just a regular person, a normal—"

"A regular person who intends to be a Marine," Bonnie said. "And who's a brown belt in karate. You *are* different, Jenny, whether you admit it or not."

"Come off it," I ordered. "What else did Drake say?"

"Let's see," said Bonnie, dragging out the words. "I asked him about himself. He says that besides running, he likes hiking. And animals—he has two dogs. He takes a lot of math and science classes, and he wants to be an engineer and build bridges. But computers bore him. Richard's supposed to be helping him with his computer work."

"I'll bet he isn't." I kicked at a rung of my chair. "Richard has never done anything to help anyone from the day he was born."

"*You* could help Drake," Bonnie pointed

out. "You could give him a copy of that book you gave Richard, the one about BASIC programming."

"You mean the one that was too simple for him, so I was a 'dumb girl' for having picked it out? I know Richard wouldn't give it back to me so I could lend it to Drake."

"No, but we could go to the mall and get another copy," Bonnie suggested.

"Do you really think that would help Drake?" I asked.

"Of course it would. But first things first. Do you think you'll still be able to go running with Drake?"

"I think I could have talked Dad into letting me do it, but Richard has already gotten him all riled up. Maybe I can change his mind, especially if I point out that its safer to run with somebody than alone."

"Good point," Bonnie agreed. Then she sighed. "What about that rotten report of Mr. Brown's? I got stuck with that snooty Marcia. Who did you get?"

"Diana," I answered, and we both groaned. "Looks like it's going to be a long semester!"

We talked a while longer before saying good night. No doubt about it, Bonnie always made me feel better. Dad might be acting weird, and Richard might be a jerk, but Bonnie never failed to cheer me up.

* * * * *

Later that night I found myself lying awake and worrying about Dad again. More than anything I wanted Mom, but I wasn't a little kid anymore. I rolled over and tried to sleep, wondering why Dad had started acting so strange. As a Marine sergeant, he had fought in wars before I was born and he'd survived. So what could be wrong now that he's a normal civilian?

After tossing and turning for a while longer, I realized I was hungry. I kept thinking about that half gallon of ice cream that I knew was in the freezer. Dad wouldn't mind if I had a bowl. I got up and found my robe and slippers. Tiptoeing past my brothers' rooms, I headed for the kitchen.

Dad was sitting at the table, slumped down in a chair. He looked up as I came in. "What's wrong, Jenny? Did you have a bad dream?"

I shook my head. "No." When I looked at the lines on Dad's face, I decided not to mention that he forgot to pick up Tim and me after karate. Dad looked old and worn-out, but he wasn't even 40 yet. "I was hungry. I thought I'd have some ice cream. Want a bowl?"

Dad sighed and picked up the package of cigarettes on the table. "No, honey. You go ahead."

My stomach started to knot up. Dad had quit smoking last year, before he lost his job at the computer company. Sometimes he threatened to start smoking again, but Mom had always talked him out of it. I noticed that half the pack was already gone. What was I going to do? It was obvious that somebody had to do something. "I wish Mom could come home. Do we really need the money that badly?"

Dad lit his cigarette. "My unemployment doesn't cut it, Jen. This Army job pays your mom more than she could make at a temporary agency. Right? We've talked and talked about this already."

"I know," I admitted. I finished dishing up my ice cream and opened the refrigerator to find the topping. That was when I saw the beer. My stomach dropped all the way to my feet. Dad used to drink a lot, but he'd promised to stop. I closed the fridge without putting anything on my ice cream. Talking to Richard hadn't worked, so the next step was in my hands. Somehow, some way, I had to get to Mom.

*   *   *   *   *

When I woke the next morning, it was barely seven. Army life started early, and Mom should be in her office by now. I grabbed my robe and pulled it on. Tying the belt, I slipped down the hall.

Richard was still snoring as I went past his room. Tim's door was shut tight, and so was Dad's. Looking cautiously over my shoulder, I headed for the kitchen and the phone extension there. I picked up the receiver and began to dial the long-distance number.

"Who are you calling at this hour?" Dad demanded from behind me.

I dropped the phone back on the hook just as it began to ring. I saw the open basement door and realized Dad had been up all night. "Dad, how come you didn't go to bed? You can't keep staying up all night."

Dad frowned at me, looking harried. "I'm the parent, Jennifer. I'll make my own decisions. I don't want you phoning your friends at this hour—it's too early. Got it?"

"Yes, sir," I said automatically, grateful that I didn't have to lie to him.

Dad nodded and went to the refrigerator. "Who is this boy that Richard was telling me about?"

I took a deep breath. "Drake Stevens. He's 15, and only a year ahead of me in school. He's the best cross-country runner on the team, and he wants me and Bonnie to run with him."

Dad opened the fridge and took out a can of beer. He popped the top and took a swallow.

I clenched my fists and felt my fingernails dig into my hands. "Do you want a glass?" Was that croak my voice? It couldn't be.

Dad eyed me. "No, thanks, honey. This is fine." He studied me with sudden amusement. "You and Bonnie, huh? Is this boy a high school kid or not?"

"Sort of," I answered. I sat on the stool by the phone, wishing I'd been able to get my call through to Mom. "The ninth graders go back and forth between the junior and senior high. Richard doesn't like Drake because he's not a computer genius. But Drake's nice. And it'll be more fun to run with friends than alone. Is it okay with you?"

Instead of answering my question, Dad looked at me strangely. He seemed to be remembering something. "I missed you and Tim last night at the *dojo*. How did you get home?"

"Sensei brought us," I answered. "Where were you, Dad?"

"I was so furious with Richard that I missed my exit on the freeway." Dad took a swallow of his beer. "The traffic was bad, and I wound up driving almost all the way to Seattle. That's a good 30 miles."

And in the wrong direction, I thought, but I didn't say that. I wouldn't talk to him about drinking beer for breakfast either. Mom would have tried to deal with it right away, but I wasn't her. Dad looked awfully guilty and I knew without being told that he'd stopped last night for a few drinks. I should have been mad at him, but I couldn't be. He was my dad. And even if he did something dumb, I still loved him. I went to him and put my arms around his waist. "I love you, Dad. It's okay."

Dad put his beer can on the table and hugged me tightly. "I'm sorry, Jen. I won't mess up like that again."

"It wasn't your fault," I said, and we stood like that for a minute. I think it made him feel better to know that I still cared about him even if he forgot to pick us up. Mom always says only robots don't make mistakes.

"Dad, can I run with Drake?"

Dad stroked my hair. "It's okay with me if that's what you want, honey. I think Richard's being a bit overprotective of you."

"Richard's just trying to make trouble," I said. "He's into arguments." I paused and looked up at Dad. "Would it be all right if

Bonnie stayed over on Friday?"

Dad chuckled. "Sure. But no snooping in the basement. I don't want you to find out about your Christmas present early."

"But, Dad!" I protested. "I already know what it is. I've been nagging for ages."

Dad looked disappointed, and I quickly hugged him. "I was only joking. I'm not going to spoil the surprise." I found myself wondering about that. Dad usually teased right back, but these days he seemed to take everything so seriously. What was the matter with him?

* * * * *

It seemed that no matter how hard I tried, I couldn't find a phone to call Mom that day. I'd been caught in my attempt in the morning, and now I decided I'd have to sneak off campus at lunchtime again and try to find a pay phone. There was one across the street at K-Mart, and if I was careful, I wouldn't get caught.

I threw my books in my locker and headed across the deserted baseball field. The sky was gray, and it seemed like it might rain. I looked around before I headed out the gate. Nobody was in sight.

"What are you doing here, Jenny?"

I must have jumped 10 feet before I turned and saw Drake coming up the sidewalk toward me. I fished for an explanation, but the words were stuck in my throat.

"Did you think I wasn't coming?" Drake asked. "I got tied up in my computer class. The teacher can't understand why I'm so dumb."

"My dad would say the problem is the teacher's." I managed to speak normally. "If he could teach, then you'd know how to operate the machine."

Drake smiled. "Thanks. I was starting to feel really stupid." He gestured toward the track. "Shall we?"

"Are you sure you want to run with me?" I asked. His smile made me feel warm all over.

Drake grinned down at me. "Only if you go slow so I can keep up."

I decided the phone call would have to wait. We went back to my locker so I could get my sweats, and it only took a few minutes to get to the gym. I changed quickly and beat Drake out to the track. I started some stretching exercises, and in a few moments Drake joined me. A person's muscles need to be warmed up properly before exercise. Richard doesn't think it's macho to warm up right. I was glad Drake had more sense.

We started slowly around the track. Drake didn't speak till we were on the second lap. "When did you decide to become a Marine? I didn't know that girls could."

"Well," I said, "I guess it's always seemed like the right thing for me. My mom's been in the Army Reserve for 20 years, and my dad had 14 years in the Marines. The military just comes naturally to me."

"I know women can be in the Army," Drake replied. "But are you sure they can be Marines?"

I started to run faster. "Of course. Women have been in the Marines since the First World War. In the beginning, it was only on reserve status and after each war, the women were discharged. But today, women make up a good part of the Corps, and they can hold all but the combat jobs. And by the way, it's not just the Army and Marines. Women can be in the Navy and the Air Force, too."

This conversation seemed a little strange to me. We were talking about a future that was at least five years away. Right now, there wasn't anywhere else I wanted to be.

* * * * *

When I got home, the house was empty.

Dad's car wasn't in the garage. I hurried to the phone, dropping my books on the kitchen table. I hoped Mom would be in the office or close to the phone.

Looking over my shoulder, I hastily dialed the number. A man answered, and I couldn't understand what he said at first. "Is Sergeant Conway there, please?"

"This is Major Morgan. Sergeant Conway is out in the field. Can I take a message?"

I wanted to cry, but I sank my teeth into my lip and fought for control. "No. I'll try again later. When will she be back?"

"Tomorrow afternoon or Saturday morning. Is this one of her kids? If it's an emergency, we'll track her down and bring her back to headquarters."

I thought about that and decided it wasn't a good idea. If Dad found out that I was causing trouble for Mom with the Army, he'd really be upset. "No, sir. I'll phone again this weekend." I hung up and tried to figure out how I'd pull that off.

Before I came up with any answers, there was a scratching at the back door. Max, our German shepherd, was asking for his dinner.

There was plenty of dry dog food, but all the canned stuff was gone. Maybe Dad was at the grocery, I thought, and will bring some home.

He says there isn't enough protein in cereal for a big animal like Max. I found the box of dog biscuits and gave Max one of those. He seemed happy for the moment, and he took the bone back outside and began to chew it.

"Anybody home?" Dad shouted from the garage. "Come help haul groceries."

I shut the back door so Max couldn't come in and escape through the garage. He always tries to get out, but then gets frightened by all the traffic in the street. "I'm here." I gathered up a sack and headed for the kitchen. "It's Richard's day for the debate team, and Tim stayed after school to help in the library. They'll come home on the activity bus."

Dad said uh-huh like he wasn't interested, but I knew if I hadn't told him where my brothers were, he'd have asked within about 30 seconds. "Did you look for work today?"

"Don't nag, Jenny. I'll find a job before my unemployment runs out."

I knew he hadn't even tried. "Do you want me to mark the ads for you like Mom does?"

Dad dumped his sack on the table. "Will you quit badgering me?" he yelled. "Bring in the groceries and put the food away!" He stormed toward the basement.

A lump rose in my throat. It hurt so badly I couldn't swallow. What was I supposed to do now? Richard wouldn't listen to me and Mom was out in the field being a soldier. Dad wasn't even pretending to look for a job. And it was turning out to be really hard to get in touch with Mom. What if I wrote her a letter? Would she believe it? Would she come home and make things right again?

I carried in the sacks of groceries and put away the food. There was all kinds of stuff, except canned meat for Max. The last thing I wanted to do was ask Dad for money, but soon Max would be scratching on the door again. I might as well get it over with and try to get back from the store before dinner. I headed for the basement.

It was pitch black down there. When I flipped the light switch at the top of the stairs, it didn't work. "Dad, it's me." I listened, but I couldn't hear anything. "Dad, are you down here?" *What a stupid question*, I thought. Of course he was. I hadn't seen him come back up.

I found the rail and reached for the next step down with my foot. "Dad?"

Nothing again. I couldn't even hear Dad's breathing. Why would he be so quiet? I finally got all the way down to the bottom and felt the cement floor under my feet. In one corner, I could see the pale gleam of the freezer. Across the room, there was the washer and dryer. In spite of myself, I looked for my Christmas present as my eyes adjusted to the darkness, but I didn't see the bulk of the castle anywhere.

Then I spotted Dad. He was over in the far corner of the basement, his back to me. He was working on something at the workbench in the light of a small utility lamp. I hurried toward him, my shoes quiet on the concrete. "Dad?" My voice seemed to lack any volume and it was almost shaking.

"You forgot Max's food." I forced myself to speak up, and the effect was awful. Dad must have jumped a foot before he spun around. In one hand, he held a pistol. And it was pointed right at me!

Four

FOR a second, Dad stood still. Then he lowered the gun till it was pointed at the floor. "My God, Jenny," he almost shouted. "Don't ever sneak up on me like that again!"

I stared at him, almost feeling my knees knock together. "Sneak up?" I sputtered. "I never sneak!" I was shaking and I realized I was very frightened. Of what? Dad would never hurt me. But sometimes it was hard to remember that this stranger was my own, real dad. "What's wrong with you?"

"Wrong with *me*?" Dad replied angrily. "What's wrong with *you*, young lady? If this gun had been loaded, I could have hurt you. When will you grow up and use your head for something besides a hat rack?"

"Hey!" I said angrily. "I didn't mean to startle you. Don't try to act like it's all *my* fault! All I wanted was some money so I could get

Max some food. You forgot it."

"No, I didn't." Dad swung around and put the gun on the workbench, and I relaxed a little. "That's why I went to the store."

"I know," I said, trying to calm down. "I wanted to feed him earlier only there wasn't any meat. I couldn't find any cans in the groceries you bought."

Dad muttered something and I was glad I didn't hear it. I looked again at the gun. Dad was breaking one of Mom's rules. She doesn't allow guns in the house. She insists that Dad keep them locked in the cabinet in the garage. When had he brought this one inside? And why?

I found myself dreading the answer to that question at the same time that I wanted to know it. "Dad, what's that gun doing here?"

"I was fixing it." Dad put an arm around me and walked me toward the stairs. "I guess I scared you, honey. I'm sorry, but you shouldn't sneak up on me like that. Not after all those years in combat when somebody creeping around meant life or death."

"You're right," I agreed, but at the same time I was pretty sure I'd made an awful lot of noise. "I'm sorry, too." I looked around again and I still didn't see my Christmas present. "Dad, where's my castle? You said you were working on it."

"I knew it!" Dad pounced on my comment like he was glad to hear something normal. He probably didn't want to think about the gun anymore either. "You're just down here to snoop." Reaching into his back pocket, he pulled out his wallet and handed me some bills. "Go get Max's food. Be back before dark. And quit coming down in the basement. You know I want to get my Christmas projects done."

"What are you making for Mom?" I asked, trying to peer around the shadowy room and into the corners. I still didn't see my castle but I did see an empty box of beer bottles.

"My favorite Christmas snoop." Dad smiled and hugged me hard. Then he turned me toward the steps. "Now, get going, Jen."

At the top of the steps, I looked back down. Dad had turned out the light I had switched on, but I thought I could see him at the bottom of the stairs. "I love you, Daddy." It may have seemed like a dumb thing to say, but just then I wanted to make sure he knew it. I had to call Mom as soon as she got back to the base. She had to know what was happening here.

* * * * *

But calling Mom didn't really seem necessary over the weekend. Dad came to watch me at karate on Friday afternoon, and he agreed that I could try for my next skill level at the rank test in two weeks. Taking a rank test costs money, so the instructor always asks the parents for permission.

After karate, we went to get Bonnie. Dad took us for pizza and then to the roller rink. As we skated, I thought about being on the track team, an idea that I'll have to admit was growing on me. *Maybe after Mom gets back home*, I thought, *maybe I can talk to her about it*. When Dad came back to pick us up after the last skating session, I had a good feeling that everything was going to be fine.

On Saturday Dad drove us to the mall, and I found a copy of the computer programming book for Drake. I still hadn't figured out how to give it to him. But I would work that out, I promised myself.

Bonnie's mom wanted to go out with her boyfriend on Saturday night, so Bonnie stayed over with me again. On Sunday afternoon we all went bowling, and Dad won. He joked and teased with us about his "superior talent." He really seemed like he was back to his normal, cheery self, and he even let Richard drive us home from the bowling alley.

Monday was pretty good, too. Diana and I went to the library to get started on our report. I wouldn't say she was friendly, but she didn't act too snobbish either. She didn't make one rude statement, which I considered rare for her. Bonnie came into the library and headed our way.

"Can I sit here?" Bonnie asked, in a low voice.

The librarian hissed at us, and I whispered, "Sure." I moved the books about Mexico. There weren't very many. Mr. Brown had assigned the reports to all his history classes, and some of the books on Mexico had already been checked out.

"This is Bonnie. And this is Diana." I introduced them, although they already knew each others' names.

The librarian made her hushing noise again and glared at us. I didn't think we were being too loud. After all, we were the only ones in the room right then. "Let's check out the books and go to the cafeteria. We can talk in there," I said.

The prospect of being seen with the two of us must have been too much for Diana. "I don't think it's going to work to do a report with you," she said stiffly. "I have to go home now." Then she stalked out.

Bonnie and I stared at each other, dumbfounded. My brothers embarrass me sometimes, but they'd never acted like that. "I'm sorry," I said.

"It wasn't your fault, Jenny." Bonnie picked up a couple of the books. "Do you want to check these out?"

"Not now. I'm going to leave them for other students to use. We'll put them back. I can come in some other time and make notes."

"Let's do it now," Bonnie opened her notebook and pulled out some paper. "You can help me with my report and I'll help you. One way or the other, you're going to have to turn in a report on Mexico, whether Diana works with you or not."

The librarian stomped over to us. "If you girls can't be quiet, then you'll have to leave."

"Yes, ma'am," I said in my most respectful tones. "I'm very sorry, ma'am. It won't happen again."

Bonnie buried her nose in the book and started coughing. I knew she was trying not to laugh, and I kicked her under the table.

"Well, you *are* the only ones here," the librarian admitted. "So you can talk—but in whispers. No loud voices. It's disrupting." She tried to smile but it was easy to see she hadn't had much practice.

"Thank you, ma'am," I said, oozing gratitude. "We really appreciate it, ma'am."

"What's this 'ma'am' stuff?" Bonnie demanded in a whisper.

"It's called *Last Word*," I explained, making sure the librarian couldn't hear. "In the military, an enlisted person always gets to say the last thing, and it can be either 'Yes, sir' or 'Yes, ma'am.' It *always* works on teachers!"

Bonnie giggled. "I'm going to try it on my mom. Maybe she'll let me visit my dad more. And I'll try it out on my aunt, too. She's awful. She always says rotten things in a sweet voice.

"Do you have to keep her as your aunt now that your mom's getting a divorce?" I asked.

Bonnie didn't say anything for a moment. Then she smiled. "I never thought about that. *Something* good could come out of this divorce if I don't have to put up with any more of my dad's creepy relatives. No more cheap bubble bath from my aunt for Christmas!"

"That's too bad," I said honestly. "The bottle you gave me killed all of Max's fleas. We've just about used it up."

"I've got three more bottles," Bonnie promised. "You can have them all."

"Thanks." And I meant it. Bonnie was a pretty special friend. I found myself wondering what she'd told Drake about me. I looked up at the library clock and realized it was almost time to meet him.

"Are you running with me today, Bonnie?"

"Not unless I have to," Bonnie decided. "Is that the only way your dad will let you do it?"

I shook my head. "No. I can make my own decision. It's okay with him."

"Good." Bonnie began to rub her leg. "Then you go run. I'm supposed to meet Marcia here, and we're going to work on our report. I'll keep making notes for you until she shows up."

"Well, if she and Diana keep being so nasty, maybe we can switch partners," I suggested. "Mr. Brown might let us. I wonder what Diana's problem was today."

"She sure did have a chip on her shoulder," Bonnie agreed. "But maybe she's always that way. Some people don't need a reason to be nasty."

"You could be right," I said. "I'll see you. I've got to hurry."

"Don't keep Drake waiting," Bonnie ordered.

"No way," I said, grinning, and headed for the door.

During my run with Drake I told him about the scene with Bonnie and Diana in the library. He started laughing when I mentioned how I'd have liked to smack Diana. "I could do it. I have a brown belt hanging in my closet and believe me, it doesn't go with my clothes."

Drake howled at the thought of my attacking Diana. "You're a lean, mean, fighting machine," he cracked.

He must have gotten that from the movies. "And you're a nerd," I retorted. Drake was right if he thought I was teasing, but I did wish he would take me a little more seriously when I talked about karate. He didn't seem to think I really had much skill. "What are you doing two weeks from Saturday?" I asked.

"Why?" Drake said. "Are you asking me out?"

"No. I want you to come to my *dojo* and see me do the rank test for my next stripe. I want you to see that learning karate is hard work."

Drake picked up on the irritation in my voice. He caught my arm and brought me to a halt. "Hey, Jenny. Mellow out. I didn't mean to make you mad."

Drake's hand was on my upper arm, and it took only one turn and one quick twist to drop him to his knees. "You didn't make me mad," I said sweetly. I headed for the girls' locker room.

When I came out, Drake was waiting. He'd gotten cleaned up and he broke into a cautious grin as he crossed the hall toward me.

He was wearing jeans and a matching sweater. He looked terrific, and I was sorry I had been angry with him.

"I guess," Drake drawled, "that you *do* know karate and that I *am* a nerd." He pulled on my wet hair. "Do I still get to come to your test?"

I nodded. "Only if you promise not to tell Sensei Larkin that I lost my temper and used a karate move on you. He'd demote me instead of promoting me."

Drake chuckled. "You didn't hurt me, Jenny. You just dented my ego."

"Maybe it needed it," I said smiling. I was relieved that he was such a good sport. "When I'm done, you'll know all about what women can and can't do."

"Yeah," Drake grinned. "So far, I know they can go into the military and learn karate. I'm improving."

"What does *your* mom do?" I asked.

"Besides the cooking, the cleaning, and the laundry?" Drake teased. He gave a cautious look. "She's an engineer. And my dad's an architect. The two of them have their own company, and they can build anything."

"Bonnie told me that you want to build bridges."

"That's right." Drake began to talk about the bridge he'd helped his uncle build during the summer. I listened closely. I'd never known bridges could be so fascinating. I'd always viewed them as just a way to get from one place to another. But for Drake, a bridge was practically a work of art. He spent a long time describing the different kinds of bridges and how they're designed.

* * * * *

I should have known better, but I found myself confiding in Richard that night. We were fixing supper, and Tim was curled up in one of the kitchen chairs reading. Dad was in the living room watching television.

"Drake says it's possible to bridge almost any distance," I said as I began to tear up lettuce for a salad.

"Yeah?" Richard forked baked potatoes into a bowl. "Well, if Drake would concentrate on computers the way he does on bridges, he might pass the programming class. He's dumb."

"No, he isn't," I flashed back. "Maybe you should be a better tutor, Richard. Sensei won't even let you lead the classes at the *dojo*, but he lets the other black belts."

"She's right," Tim glanced up from his book. "Sensei Larkin says you don't have any patience, and that's what you need to learn to become a master."

Richard slammed the bowl of potatoes on the table and came over to where I'd started to cut tomatoes. "Go get Dad. I'll finish the salad. And I'll try to be more patient with your stupid boyfriend."

"He's not my boyfriend," I protested. But I saw the look Tim gave me, and I knew I was going to hear about it for the next couple of days.

Dad was in his favorite chair with his back to the wall. The television newscaster was talking about trouble in the Mideast, but Dad wasn't paying attention. He was sound asleep.

I tiptoed to the TV and turned it off. Then I took an afghan from the couch and covered Dad with it. He sighed and slipped deeper into sleep, almost snoring. It seemed like the most beautiful sound in the world.

Dad hadn't gone to bed for days. At night he went to the basement. When Tim asked him why, Dad mumbled something about nightmares. Well, tonight Dad didn't seem to be having bad dreams.

I headed back to the kitchen. "Dad's zonked. Let's eat without him."

Richard gave me an exasperated look. "And what's he going to say when he wakes up? He won't be happy about it, I'll tell you that much."

"I'll tell him I decided to let him rest," I said. "He won't blame you."

"I'll still be the oldest," Richard retorted, "and I think he won't like it if we let him sleep through dinner. Go wash up, Tim. *I'll* get Dad."

I followed Richard as he stormed into the living room and grabbed Dad's shoulder, giving him a rough shake.

In an instant, Dad had seized Richard's wrist. He bore down hard, forcing Richard to his knees. Richard turned white, and I thought he was going to pass out. Then I realized Dad hadn't even opened his eyes. I was really scared.

"No!" I shouted. "Dad, don't!" I ran across the room. "Let him go, Dad." I tried to pry Dad's fingers off Richard's wrist but his grip was like steel. I was almost crying. "Dad, please. Dad?"

Five

"JENNY, what's wrong?" Dad opened his eyes and stared at me.

I caught my breath. "Dad, let Richard go! You're hurting him."

Dad glanced down at Richard as if he'd never seen him before, and then he did let go. "Are you all right, Richard?"

"Yes, sir." Richard was rubbing his wrist. "I came to get you for dinner and I guess I startled you, sir."

Dad tossed the blanket toward the couch and got to his feet. "Well, let's eat. I'm starved." He paused. "Next time, speak to me first, Richard. Don't just grab me."

"Yes, sir," Richard agreed quickly.

Dad started out of the room and I looked up at Richard. "I think we'd better call Mom. He's really weirding out."

Richard rubbed his wrist some more. "That

was all my fault. I should have spoken to him first. Dad's right. And we aren't calling Mom. There's nothing to call her about."

He's wrong this time, I thought. I was going to call Mom and I would tell her the entire story. Something was different about Dad. He'd never acted like this before. That thought stayed with me the next day. I had to talk to Mom. I had made my decision.

I got through my morning classes okay. When noon came, Diana wasn't around and neither was Drake. I wanted to go to a nearby store with a pay phone and call Mom, but I didn't want to miss my running date with Drake. If I hurried, there would be plenty of time. I went through my usual routine of stuffing my books in the locker before I headed across the school grounds.

For once there wasn't a long line at the pay phone. Now, how was I going to place the call? If I charged the call to the Army, they wouldn't want to pay for it, and Mom would get in trouble. I decided to put it on our bill at home.

I dialed the operator and explained that I wanted to place a long-distance call to California.

"How do you want to bill this call?" the woman asked.

"To my home number." I gave it to her. So

far, so good.

"Is there someone at that number who can verify that you can place this call?"

I stared at the pay phone as though it had just sprung from a horror movie. "I don't understand."

"You have to have somebody's permission to bill the call to a residential number," the woman explained. "Is somebody home to say it's okay to charge the cost of the long-distance call there?"

Dad, I thought. No way should he know about this call. "Never mind," I said, and hung up. Now, what? I *had* to talk to Mom. Was there somebody I could charge the call to who would verify it for the operator? Grandma?

Forget it, I thought. If there's something wrong with Dad, the last thing Mom would want is for all the relatives to know. I needed to talk to her, but I simply couldn't tell anyone else about it.

Trying to think of a way out of this mess, I headed back to school. This time, my luck ran out. Mr. Nichols, the vice principal, caught me at the gate.

He frowned at me. "Are you allowed off campus, Jennifer?"

"No, sir," I said, and wished I were good at lying. What kind of story could I give him?

I didn't have to make one up. Mr. Nichols lectured me royally, but he didn't drag me off to his office or call Dad. He took up most of my lunchtime and then told me to go to my next class. I was glad I'd scraped through with just a warning, but I'd still have to come up with another plan to call Mom. And it had to be a plan that wouldn't get me in more trouble at school.

I hurried to the gym and looked for Drake. He wasn't there, and I didn't see him on the outdoor track either. When I went back inside, he was just coming out of the boys' locker room. "I'm sorry I didn't make it today," I said. I started to explain, but Drake just glared at me. He wasn't listening.

He fished in his pocket and yanked out a quarter. He threw it to me, and I caught it. "Next time you decide to stand me up, call me. Then I won't have to waste my time waiting for you."

Before I could say anything, he was gone. I held the quarter in my hand and slumped down on one of the benches in the hall. Phys ed was my next class, but I didn't feel like dressing or taking part. Drake was mad at me. Mr. Nichols would be watching me. Dad was acting strange. Everybody thought *I* was a troublemaker. And I still hadn't gotten through to Mom. What else could possibly go wrong?

That afternoon when I got home, Dad was back in the basement. He yelled something about working on Christmas projects and wanting to be left alone. I found myself wondering whether he was actually working on projects or simply sitting down there with another six-pack of beer.

I didn't ask. Instead, I slumped into the living room and turned on the television. Usually, I can find something to do besides watching TV. But today I was too miserable to play with Max or rearrange the furniture in one of my dollhouses, or even practice my routines for the upcoming karate test.

I thought about calling Bonnie, but I couldn't come up with anything cheerful to say. The last thing she needed was to have me whine at her about all my troubles. *And let's face it*, I thought. *Bonnie doesn't know any more about boys than I do. She can't give me advice about Drake.*

Mom could. Before I knew it, I was back in the kitchen, dialing the number in California. I hoped Dad would stay in the basement, but I didn't have any guarantees. Mom answered the phone on the second ring.

"Mom, this is Jenny. Everything's going

wrong up here. Dad's freaked out and I had a fight with Drake and—"

"Slow down, Jennifer," Mom said cheerfully. "Who is Drake?"

"A boy I go running with. Only I was trying to call you during lunch and I was late to go running and he got mad. What do I do?"

"Write him off," Mom advised. "If he gets mad that easily, he can't be worth it."

"I don't want to write him off," I protested. "I really like him. He's interesting, and funny—and he knows *everything* about building bridges—"

"Building bridges, huh?" Mom thought a minute. "Give him time to calm down, and then build a bridge *to him*. Talk to him, honey. Communicate. Tell him why you were late, and that you're sorry."

I laughed. Mom is big on communication. But she's usually right about it. "I love you, Mom," I told her. "We miss you."

"I miss you, too," Mom said, and I knew she meant it. "How are you and Richard getting along? Still fighting?"

"No more than usual," I said honestly. I hesitated. Why did this feel so much like snitching on Dad? "Richard's okay, and so is Tim. It's Dad I'm worried about. He's really on edge."

Mom sighed. "I know that, Jenny. Every time your dad loses a job, he loses some of his pride along with it. You should understand that it's very hard for him when I'm working and he isn't. Cut him some slack, sweetheart. He'll get a job and then he'll be fine."

"He's not even looking for a job," I continued doggedly. "He's smoking again and he's drinking, too. He doesn't sleep either, and he told Tim he's having nightmares. Mom, something's wrong."

"Jennifer, your father's a grown man. Grown-ups sometimes have difficult times, like kids do. The best we can do is offer our support and let him make his own decisions. He'll work it out. You've just got to hang in there with him."

"Will you talk to him?" I asked. "If you could just hear his voice, maybe you'd realize I'm telling the truth."

"Jenny, I don't doubt you at all. I just think you're taking too much of this problem on yourself. Go get him. Where is he?"

"In the basement. Just a minute." I put the phone on the counter and ran to the downstairs door. Yanking it open, I shouted, "Dad, Mom's on the phone and she wants to talk to you."

Dad came up, his breath smelling of beer.

But Mom couldn't tell that over the phone, could she? I knew it was rude to listen, but I didn't care. Would Mom know I wasn't exaggerating after she heard him?

Dad grabbed the receiver and clutched it so hard I thought it would break. "Hi, honey. Glad you called. What's going on?"

I couldn't hear what Mom said, but I didn't think she'd give me away. Dad frowned at me and waved me toward the door to the living room. "I want to talk to her again," I insisted.

"Then I'll call you when I'm done," Dad said, pulling away from the receiver for a moment.

It was 15 minutes by the clock over the TV before Dad yelled for me to come take the phone. He was grinning as he started for the basement, and I heard him whistling on his way down the stairs. Whatever Mom had said certainly did the trick, I thought.

"Well?" I asked. "What do you think?"

Mom sounded a little concerned. "You'd better write me a letter and tell me everything that's been happening up there, Jennifer. Your dad does sound kind of down. Should I give up the tour and come home now?"

I looked at the calendar and mentally counted the days. "You'll be through in less than three weeks won't you? I think it'll be okay till then. Could you call more often? Especially during the daytime when Dad's here alone?"

"Yes," Mom promised. "I will. I've got to get back to work now, honey. Write me that letter. And be patient with your dad. He said he'd start reading the ads again, and go on interviews. Once he gets a job, I'm sure he'll be all right. I love you. Take care of things till I get home."

After she hung up, tears burned in my eyes. I knew Mom felt responsible for finishing her tour, but three more weeks did seem like a long time. Did she really understand how bad Dad is? Or did he manage to cover it up when they talked? And what if Mom was wrong— what if the problem is bigger than just finding a job?

Right after Dad left the Marines, he'd gone to work for a big plane manufacturer. When there was a slump in the economy, he'd been laid off. That hadn't been his fault, not really. Then he'd been a manager in a warehouse for Providence Hospital down in Seattle. His boss had given him a hard time, and Dad never was much good at hiding his opinions. Dad had quit at the same time that his boss fired him.

After a while, Dad had found a new job at a computer manufacturing company. He'd stayed there till last year when something awful had happened, and they fired him. Dad wouldn't tell us kids what the problem was, and Mom refused to talk about it, too. Since then, Dad had stayed home and drawn unemployment. Mom had worked off and on as a computer operator for a temporary-help agency.

I glared at the telephone, trying to swallow my disappointment that calling Mom hadn't instantly made everything right. After all, what had I expected her to do? Fix Dad as if he were a broken toy?

I heard the knock on the front door and jumped up, relieved to have a distraction from my problems.

To my surprise, it was Diana. She had her arms full of books. "Hi," I said.

"Hi," Diana said back. "I brought these over and I thought we could get started outlining our report." She seemed to have forgotten her stormy exit from the school library a few days before.

"Come on in." I held the door wide and grabbed for some of the texts. "Did you go back to the school library?"

"No. My mom took me downtown to the public library. They had a lot more stuff on Mexico. Our report will be the best in the class."

Her attitude sure had changed. I led the way into the kitchen and we put the books on the table. "Would you like a mineral water? Or a glass of milk? Or something?"

Diana gave me a funny look. "What about a soda?"

I shook my head. "Sorry. My dad's into healthy stuff. He says there are too many chemicals in junk food. We have seltzer, and that tastes a little like cola."

Diana shrugged. "Okay. I'll try it."

I opened the refrigerator and pulled out two of the little bottles. "When I stay over with Bonnie," I said, "we go for potato chips and a six-pack of cola. My dad doesn't get too upset about pizza. He says it's healthy. But burgers are forbidden. Mom still takes us to McDonald's, though."

I was talking too much and I knew that. But Diana made me nervous. She's one of the most popular girls in school, and she has a million friends. I just have Bonnie. But of course, Bonnie's a *good* friend, and that's better than a ton of the other kind, according to Mom.

Diana sat down in one of the kitchen chairs and reached for the book on top of the stack. "I thought we could outline the entire thing and then choose the parts we each like best.

What do you think?"

"That sounds great. You make it sound possible. When Mr. Brown was talking about all the points we had to cover, it seemed like a pretty big chore." I sat down across from Diana and picked up the next book off the top of the stack. This was going to take a while, but I was glad Diana had come over. Finally we would make some progress on that darned report.

About an hour later we were halfway through the books. I was starved, and I was sure Diana was too. But as I'd told her, we didn't have any potato chips or snacks like that. "Would you like some popcorn?" I asked.

Diana smiled. "Yes. Do you need some help?"

"Nope. Our popper's a little old-fashioned. I'd better do it." I fished the metal contraption out of a lower cupboard and plugged it in, quickly adding oil and then a scoop of popcorn before I slammed the lid on.

The corn began to sizzle and finally started popping and banging against the lid, making a lot of racket. The aroma of hot popcorn filled the air. I wasn't surprised when I heard Dad coming up from the basement.

Remembering how happy he'd seemed after talking to Mom, I called out to him as he came up the stairs. "Hey, Dad! Want some popcorn?"

But he was totally changed. To my amazement, Dad stormed across the kitchen, never stopping to say hello to Diana, and grabbed the corn popper, yanking the cord out of the socket. Muttering angrily, he dumped the whole thing into the trash. Then, without a word, he stomped out of the room, leaving the two of us stunned and silent.

Six

DIANA couldn't leave fast enough, and I didn't blame her. When Dad behaved strangely around the family it was one thing. But when he carried on in front of guests, it was something else entirely. I stormed into my bedroom and slammed the door, embarrassed and confused.

Mom wanted a letter and by heaven, I was going to write her one. I'd list all the weird things Dad had done, from almost breaking Richard's arm to this latest scene.

How could I face going back to school? I was sure that Diana would tell all of her friends about the popcorn popper. She was probably on the phone right now, I thought. The story would sweep the school in no time.

I was on the third page of my letter to Mom when I heard the knock on my door. "Who is it?"

"Me," Richard said as he came in. "What's wrong? Dad said you were in here sulking. He wants you to come to dinner."

I swung around on my chair and glared at him. "Dad just embarrassed me in front of Diana. He just blew up for no reason when we were trying to fix popcorn. I don't care what *you* think about him. *I* think he's going around the bend."

Richard had come over to my desk, and he looked down at the first page of my letter. "So, you're going to write to Mom and scare the heck out of her? Do you really think she needs to hear about all this when she can't do anything about it?"

"Well, I'm not going to have all this happening and not try to do something," I retorted. Before I could stop him, Richard grabbed all three pages of my letter.

I went after him, but Richard held the letter out of reach. "Give it back. That's mine," I shouted.

"What's going on here?" Dad demanded from the doorway. "Are you two fighting again?"

"No, sir," Richard said. He tore my letter into several pieces and threw them into the wastebasket.

"Jennifer?" Dad asked, looking at me.

I glowered back at him. Mom had always said Dad and I are a lot alike, but I can't see it. I'd never point a gun at somebody, or try to break Richard's arm, or throw the popcorn popper into the garbage. Who was this stranger I was supposed to be a lot like? "We aren't fighting, sir. And now I'd like to be alone, sir."

"Dinner's almost ready," Dad said gently. I couldn't believe it. His mood had changed again. "Come eat, honey. You'll feel better."

"Why should I? Are you going to throw another appliance into the garbage, and you need an audience?" All my anger was pouring out of me now. Dad frowned at me like I was a little kid throwing a tantrum, but I didn't care. "Or are you going to wait till I have another friend over and embarrass me again? Is that what I have to look forward to?"

"Jennifer, calm down," Dad ordered in a hard voice. "You know the sound of that popper irritates me."

"It never did before," I flung back. "And what else was I supposed to serve for a snack? We aren't allowed to have real food like other kids."

Now Dad looked really irritated. He planted his fists on his hips and said sternly, "Straighten up, Jennifer Marie Conway, or you'll be grounded until you're 18."

"Try it," I shouted. "Mom will be home in three weeks and she won't allow it."

"Excuse me, sir." Richard edged past him and out the door. "I'll go finish fixing supper."

Dad sat down on the bed. I stared at my desk where the letter had been. For about five minutes, neither of us said anything. I could hear Richard banging around in the kitchen.

"I'm sorry, Jen," Dad finally said in a calm voice. "I shouldn't have lost my temper earlier, so I won't blame you for losing yours now. It's just that the noise of that popper was driving me crazy. I couldn't take it. I didn't mean to embarrass you in front of your friend."

I couldn't stay mad at Dad. "I'm sorry, too, Dad. I was rude just now. I shouldn't have yelled those things at you."

Dad chuckled suddenly. "You have more guts than your brothers. They'd never fight back like that." He held out his arms. "Come give me a hug, honey. I may not deserve it, but I need one."

I ran across the room and hugged him hard. "Do you really think I'm brave? Sometimes I get so scared, and that worries me. What kind of a Marine will I be if I get frightened easily?"

Dad stroked my hair. "Well, we don't really have to worry about that. You're a girl, thank heavens. It isn't likely you'll ever really join the Marines."

I stepped back a little and looked up at him in shock. How could he forget that enlisting in the Marines was my dream? It had been since I was a little kid. "But I thought you wanted us to go into the military!"

Dad tipped up my chin with his hand. "I'm not so sure a military career will bring you happiness," he said. "I know I've held that up before you as the best kind of life. And your mother is a success in the Reserve. But I'm not so sure that I really want my kids to be career officers. It's a tough life." He looked away from me. "It can cause you a lot of grief. Right now, I'd rather have you look at the other kinds of things you can do with your life."

I couldn't believe what I was hearing. This new change in Dad's attitude made the corn-popper incident look like everyday behavior! I felt shaken and uncertain. Had Dad changed his mind about this just because I'm a girl? Or was he questioning the military life because of his own problems? Either way, did it mean I should give up *my* dream?

I hugged Dad again, and we went downstairs to eat. Our dinner table had never been as quiet as it was that evening.

* * * * *

School the next day was awful. I'd no sooner walked into history class than Mr. Brown signaled me. I went up to his desk. "Yes, sir?"

"Jenny, is there some problem with your working with Diana?" Mr. Brown looked at me and waited for an answer.

"No, sir," I responded. "I thought we were doing fine."

"I see." Mr. Brown looked puzzled.

I didn't want to try to explain everything. "We've had some problems," I said, "but I think things are getting better."

"All right," Mr. Brown replied, still looking worried. "I want you two to work out your differences even if you never really get to be friends."

"I'll try, sir." Fortunately, it was time for class to start. When the lecture was over, I slipped out before Mr. Brown could say anything more to me.

Bonnie was waiting when I got to our locker. She seemed upset, and I wondered whether her parents' divorce was getting to her again. "What's wrong?" I asked.

Bonnie took a deep breath. "That rotten Diana. She's telling everybody that your dad is really weird."

"Well, I expected that," I said, putting my books away. "But what can I do? I can't very well punch her out." *Besides*, I thought, *Diana isn't far from being right . . . even if she shouldn't be blabbing it all over school.*

I wondered what Bonnie had heard. "Dad got irritated by the noise the popcorn popper was making yesterday afternoon," I explained. "He threw the whole thing into the trash. Diana was sitting right there."

Bonnie's eyes widened. "That must have been quite a scene."

"Well, it was," I admitted. "But it's over now. I guess I'll just have to live with whatever people are saying." I hoped that would be the end of it, but I couldn't deny my hurt. Whoever made up that rhyme about "sticks and stones will break your bones" was wrong about the part that says "words will never hurt you." Words *do* hurt. And I was feeling it.

* * * * *

It was lunchtime, and Bonnie and I headed for the cafeteria. As we went through the doors we saw Diana coming toward us. She was with a couple of cheerleaders, and she stopped to glare at me. "I don't know what you told Mr. Brown, but your dad is awful."

I felt my temper starting to flare up. I remembered that Dad always said I should rule my emotions instead of letting them rule me. And Sensei told me the same thing. "My dad's okay," I replied. "He's just having a hard time since he lost his job."

Diana sniffed. "Well, my dad never lost a job. But it's obvious *your* dad has got real problems. It's no wonder he's unemployed!"

From the corner of my eye, I saw Bonnie stiffen. I knew she was about to say something nasty, so I elbowed her. Bonnie's become very loyal to my family, especially since her parents are divorcing. "My dad was a Marine for a long time. Sometimes he has a hard time dealing with civilians," I explained.

Diana gave me her haughtiest look. "*My* dad was a soldier, too, and he even fought in Vietnam."

"For heaven's sake, Diana," I snapped. "Can't you just mellow out? My dad was having a bad day and you just saw part of it. I suppose your father never has bad days either?"

That shut her up. Her face started to go white, and I realized I had gone too far. Before I could apologize she was gone.

"That was pretty rude," one of the cheerleaders said.

"So was she," Bonnie retorted. "And if I had a brown belt in karate like Jenny does, I'd have introduced her to the floor!"

That took care of the cheerleaders. They headed for the gym. I knew they would probably keep blabbing, but at least I wouldn't have to hear it. "I didn't mean to hurt Diana," I said to Bonnie. "Looks like she can dish it out, but she can't take it."

"Well, wait a while before you go apologize," Bonnie ordered. "She should have a chance to think this over."

"How did you know I was thinking of apologizing?" I demanded. "Sometimes I think you can read my mind!"

"I've known you for six years," Bonnie retorted. "You always feel guilty when you hurt someone's feelings even if they've hurt yours worse."

Bonnie was right, I thought. I felt guilty for getting mad at Dad when he did odd things. I couldn't even stand to let a fight with Richard go on very long. I wondered if my Mom felt the same way when she was angry with someone. I would have to talk to her about that when she got home, I thought.

*   *   *   *   *

That afternoon when I got home from karate, I headed for my room. As usual, Dad was down in the basement. I had a lot to do, with the rank test coming up soon. I needed to practice all my *katas* at least twice a day. And my karate uniform was really filthy. It would have to be washed and pressed carefully. And that isn't as easy as it sounds. The *gi* and belt are made of old-fashioned cotton fabric—not exactly permanent press!

I took the uniform and belt to the basement and threw them in the washer. I selected cold water for both cycles and added the right amount of soap. As soon as the machine stopped, I'd have to pull out my *gi* and hang it up.

Richard and Tim were lucky. They could forget about wearing T-shirts under the jacket of their uniforms. But girls have to add a T-shirt because of the way that the uniform top closes so loosely in front—it doesn't have any buttons either.

Thinking about that and the right color T-shirt to wear for the test, I went back to my room. Dad never even looked up from his corner workbench the whole time I was in the basement. I wished Mom were here. Just knowing she was rooting for me had given me confidence on other tests.

I really wanted to do well and get to the next level of brown belt. Tim was catching up to me fast in karate, and I'd never live it down if he made black belt before I did. At least *he* wouldn't let me hear the end of it, and neither would Richard.

I'd no sooner found a light brown T-shirt in my bureau than the phone rang. It was Bonnie. I curled up on the stool by the kitchen extension and we talked about school for a while.

"What I really called for is to find out about Drake," Bonnie chirped. "How are you two doing?"

"We aren't," I said. "I got caught by Mr. Nichols the other day when I was sneaking back on campus. I was still trying to call Mom. Anyway, Nichols lectured me *forever*. By the time I got to the gym to meet Drake for running, it was almost one o'clock. Drake was really mad, and he wouldn't let me explain. So, I guess it's over. Unless I can think of a way to make up with him."

"No way," Bonnie squawked. "If he won't even let you explain, he's a jerk. It wasn't your fault. If he wants to make up, *he* should be the one to apologize."

I had to admit I liked her advice. It made me feel better to know that for once, I wasn't going to feel guilty over something I wasn't to blame for. Bonnie and I talked a while longer, and then it was time to start supper. After dinner I worked on my history report and other homework.

It was after I'd gone to bed that I remembered my uniform. I jumped up and headed for the washer. If my *gi* and my belt were still wet, they wouldn't crease as badly. Ironing them wouldn't be so hard.

But my *karate-gi* wasn't in the washer. Neither was the belt. They weren't hanging in the bathroom either. I opened the door to Richard's room. "Have you seen my *gi*? I forgot and left it in the washing machine."

Richard shook his head, not lifting his eyes from the book on computer languages. "No. Tim wanted to do a load, and I think Dad was helping him. Did you check the dryer?"

I stared at him and felt my stomach tighten. "Tim knows better than to dry a uniform. Sensei has told us not to a hundred times."

Richard stood up from his desk. "We'd better look in the dryer. Mom dried my *gi* back when I first started karate. The world didn't come to an end."

Sure enough, my uniform was in the dryer. And so was my belt—or what remained of it. The wide, brown material was all shrunk and withered up so that it looked like a twisted snake. The uniform wasn't shrunk as badly, but it was definitely smaller and the white pants and jacket were splattered with brown dots.

If Richard hadn't been there, I'd have cried. I knew Tim hadn't thrown my uniform in the dryer. Dad had done it. How *could* he? After all the years we'd been in karate, he should know better.

I was a goner. Sensei Larkin had always insisted that each student take responsibility for his or her uniform. He didn't want to hear any excuses. If I wore these rags to class, he'd never let me take the rank test. He'd probably demote me. I dumped the uniform on the floor and ran for my room, leaving Richard standing in the basement, shaking his head.

Seven

FRIDAY was my next karate class, and I did work up the courage to go after all. I hadn't intended to after the laundry disaster on Wednesday, but the test was only one week away. I needed the practice. I couldn't wear my uniform, so I took my newest pair of sweats.

Sensei Larkin's eyebrows shot clear up to his hairline when he saw me. Everybody else was in *gi*'s. And my blue pants and shirt made me stand out like a sore thumb.

"Jennifer, be in my office after class," Sensei ordered as he passed by me, and then he went on to the next person.

We were practicing leg positions for our kicks, always my worst exercise. Today I didn't dare to mess up at all. I knew Sensei was watching closely for every error.

On Fridays we also have to review all our

katas from the beginning routines to the advanced ones. I had to do all 38 of mine plus the two new ones. Sensei Larkin stood glaring at me and waited like a vulture for my mistakes. I had to redo three of my routines.

After class, I went to his office as he had ordered. I got there even before he did. When Sensei came in, I bowed and murmured the proper greeting. How could Dad set me up for all this trouble?

Sensei Larkin looked even sterner than usual. "What is the proper uniform for class, Jennifer?"

"A clean *karate-gi* with the right *obi* to show one's rank, Sensei."

"Where is yours?"

I took a deep breath. "I was washing it, and my dad did a dumb thing. He threw it in the dryer. By the time I found out, it was too late. The *obi* is ruined, and the *gi* is so small that even Tim couldn't wear it."

"It wasn't your father's uniform," Sensei said, correcting me. "It was yours. *You* didn't take care of it. We cannot blame others for our own failures." He looked at me very hard. "Now. What is the rule about parents, Jennifer?"

"One should honor and respect one's parents," I recited. The rule had been drilled into us, so I knew Sensei expected me to get it right.

"Is blaming your failure on your father an example of honoring him?"

I shook my head miserably. I was close to tears. Sensei was silent for a moment, as if he were reviewing the situation.

"I'll find you a new *gi* and belt," he said. "You're to do 10 push-ups for the uniform. Fifteen for the belt. And 15 knuckle push-ups for the lack of respect for your father."

The punishment was a tough one. I was almost ready to protest when I remembered how much trouble Richard had gotten into with Mom and Dad when he argued with Sensei. So I bowed and muttered, "*Oss*, Sensei."

Forty push-ups and it was all Dad's fault. I almost hated him. I left the office and went back to the classroom to get started.

I was still doing push-ups when Dad arrived to pick us up. Tim, who had been waiting in the parking lot, came back inside and squatted down beside me. "Dad wants to know when you'll be ready to go home."

"Twenty more push-ups," I puffed and kept cranking them out. This many push-ups would be nearly impossible for most girls, but Sensei makes us do 125 just to warm up when we start class. And you have to do push-ups and sit-ups to qualify for a new belt or level.

"Dad's getting pretty impatient," Tim warned.

I looked for Sensei Larkin before I spoke. "Well, this is all *his* fault," I said in a low voice. "He can just wait."

Tim shrugged. "I'll go tell him that you'll be out after about 10 more push-ups, and after you get your new uniform, and after Sensei lectures you some more."

Unfortunately, Tim was right about what it was going to take to get out of there. I finally finished the push-ups. Then I got my new uniform, and Sensei gave me another slow, stern lecture.

Dad scowled at me when I got in the car. "What took you so long?"

"Nothing," I snapped back and slammed the rear car door.

Dad glared at me as he started the engine. "What's your problem, now?"

"Nothing, *sir*!"

"Don't play Last Word with me, young lady!"

I shut up and didn't say another word the rest of the way home. If I never spoke to Dad again, it would be too soon, I thought. How was I ever going to get through the next two weeks till Mom came home?

I could hear the phone ringing as we walked in. I hurried to answer it, not surprised that it was Bonnie. Hearing her voice made me want to have a long talk with her.

"Bonnie, can I stay over with you tonight?"

"Sure. Just a minute and I'll ask my mom."

"Ask her for tomorrow night, too. I've got a big problem, and you have to help me."

"Hmmm. This sounds interesting," Bonnie said. "Just a second."

She was back on the line in a few minutes. Her mom would come get me in an hour. Now all I had to do was get Dad's permission. He had gone to the basement as soon as we got home, and I gave him time to get busy with a project while I packed some stuff for the weekend. Then I went to the head of the stairs and called down to ask. As I had expected, Dad agreed. I made a point of telling both Richard and Tim where I was so that when Dad surfaced, they could remind him that he had said it was okay.

Bonnie's mom arrived on schedule and drove us back to their apartment. She had a date that evening, and seemed glad that I would be there with Bonnie. As soon as she was gone, I looked at Bonnie. "I do need your help, really."

"What's wrong? Is it Drake?"

"No, it's my dad. He's gotten really strange. I told you about the popcorn popper, but that isn't all. He acts crazy a lot, and he doesn't remember things, and he gets mad so easily!"

Bonnie twisted a strand of hair around her finger and her blue eyes showed concern. Once I'd started talking, it was hard to stop. I told her about Dad's nightmares, about the way he'd ruined my karate uniform, and how he'd said I shouldn't go into the Marines.

Bonnie was so sympathetic, I wished I had talked to her long ago. She suggested that I write the letter to my mom right then. That way, Richard wouldn't have a chance to tear it up. We started the letter that night, and worked on it all weekend.

I knew that Mom was expecting the letter from me, and it was a load off my mind when we slipped it into the downtown mailbox on Sunday afternoon. *Now*, I thought, *Mom can figure out whatever it is that's wrong with Dad.* I could concentrate on my karate test, my history report, and the problem with Drake—not necessarily in that order!

* * * * *

Dad was pretty mellow the next week. He remembered to pick us up after karate class, but he was still spending a lot of time in the basement. I wondered if Mom would call after she got my letter.

I kept looking for Drake around school all week, but with no luck. I spent a lot of time at the gym, thinking he would *have* to come there, but he seemed to be making himself pretty scarce. I wanted to ask Richard about him, but didn't dare. Richard would make too much of it, and might even tell Drake I was looking for him.

On Saturday morning, I had to be at the *dojo* early. Richard got the keys to Dad's car and drove me downtown. He promised to try to get Dad there on time for my rank test. I went in and changed into my *gi*. Then I began to warm up, jumping rope and doing some stretching exercises.

Sensei Larkin came in and helped me with my kicks. He tested me on four of my *katas*, and I forgot a couple of the movements. The superstition said that a bad rehearsal meant a good rank test, so I wasn't too scared.

The first part of the test was really just qualifications. It was easy for me to do the required push-ups and sit-ups, as well as the two stances. Now, I was ready for the part that tests sparring abilities. I did pretty well on that, too, but nobody was there to cheer me on. What had happened to my brothers and my dad?

In a way, I was glad that Richard had missed the sparring. I had to go up against one of the boys, and we performed a mock fight. In this exercise, the blows don't really connect, and nobody is supposed to get hurt. But Richard had been there at my first bout some months ago when I messed up and did the wrong block. I had gotten a badly bruised arm. Richard thought my opponent had hit me on purpose, and he tried to beat up the kid. Sensei was furious, and Dad had to talk him out of giving Richard a heavy penalty. I think that Dad was secretly a little proud of Richard, even if he *had* lost his temper.

I was sitting with some of the other students when Richard and Tim finally arrived. I didn't see Dad. Was he parking the car? I went to ask.

Richard looked upset as he came closer. "Dad's put a lock on the basement door, and he's not coming up. I must have called down there a dozen times. I think you're right about telling Mom."

"We came on the bus," Tim offered. "The car's at home, and if Dad changes his mind maybe he'll come. We left him a note. I'm sorry, Jenny. I know you wanted him here. We weren't fighting with him or anything."

"It isn't your fault," I managed to say, but I felt the tears catching in my throat. Richard rested a hand on my shoulder, and I knew he was trying to comfort me. "I already wrote to Mom," I said.

"Well, let's call her anyway," Richard said. "We can tell her that you've got your second-level brown belt."

"I might not get it," I reminded him. "All that's left is the *kata* part of the test but it's the most important. If I make a mistake, I'm out."

"You'll do fine," Richard assured me.

I forced my eyes open further, trying not to cry. When I glanced past Richard, I saw Drake. He seemed a little nervous, but he gave me a broad grin when I noticed him. I pulled away from my brother and went to meet Drake. "Hi."

"Hello," Drake said quietly. "Are you mad at me? I deserve it."

I shook my head. "No." I could feel butterflies dancing inside me, and I didn't know whether it was because of him or the test. "I wanted to tell you why I was late, but I never got the chance."

Drake looked around the room that was crowded with students and teachers. "It's too noisy to talk in here. Can you come outside?"

"We'll have to talk later," I said with regret. "We're almost ready to start the hardest part of the test. And I can't break any more of Sensei's rules. I'm not real popular with him already."

Drake laughed. "Is he the guy who made me take off my shoes when I came in?"

"That's him," I agreed. I took Drake over to where Richard and Tim were sitting. Richard started explaining how karate works. I realized he was trying to be nice.

Now all I had left to do was explain to Sensei Larkin that Dad wasn't coming. It's generally expected you'll have your parents come when you take a test. Sensei says it shows respect to your parents and to the school as well.

Sensei Larkin was in his office talking to another student's parents, so I waited outside in the hall till he was done.

"Is something wrong, Jenny?"

"My dad is having a bad day and he won't be able to come." I got all choked up and wanted to cry, but I was determined not to do it in front of my karate instructor.

"Well, he already gave permission for you to take the test," Sensei Larkin said slowly. "And your mother told me she'd pay the test fee when she gets home. So, all we have to decide is whether you feel like doing the rank test today or at a later time."

Sensei wanted me to have the choice of waiting if I felt I wouldn't perform as well without my dad there. I thought quickly, but decided not to wait. "Let's do it now," I said.

My teacher smiled and put an arm around my shoulders. "You're a good *karate-ka*, Jennifer."

I knew he meant I was a good student, and I thanked him for the compliment. Richard claims I'm one of Sensei's favorites, but I don't think so. Sensei is harder on me than he is on anybody else, even the boys. I have to work super-hard for his praise.

Rank tests are never easy. There are three teachers who watch a student perform the routines. I'll never forget my first test. I was told to do a certain *kata*, and I did the wrong one. So then they told me to do that one, and I did a different one. I got my orange belt anyway, but that was when I was 10. Today, there weren't any excuses. Sensei had already offered to let me do the test another time.

Today I wanted to do well, especially with Drake in the audience. When my turn finally came, I took a deep breath and went to the middle of the room. I bowed to the teachers who were acting as the judges.

The oldest one told me what routine to do. I took another deep breath, bowing again, before I announced my name and the *kata*. It began with a block, and from there every movement flowed into the next. I didn't forget a single blow, kick, or block. I performed the entire routine without glancing at Drake or my brothers.

I finished at precisely the point on the floor where I'd begun, and I bowed to the judges again. I expected them to ask for another *kata*, but they didn't. That was very unusual. The three judges just put their heads together and spoke for a moment. I remained standing in the center of the performance floor. In a moment, the judge who was the spokesman came out of the huddle and said I was dismissed.

That seemed like very bad news. I thought I must have totally misjudged how well my *kata* had gone. It had seemed to flow! Were there errors I wasn't ever aware of? How bad could it have been for the judges to dismiss me without even asking for a second *kata*?

I walked over to join my brothers and Drake on the benches at the side of the room. Richard looked perplexed, but Tim was practically jumping up and down. "That was great,

Jenny!" he was repeating. "You're really good!"

"I don't need to hear that right now," I snapped. I slumped onto the floor. "I was awful, wasn't I?"

Drake put his hand on my shoulder. "I thought you were great, but I don't know anything about karate except what I see on television."

"It actually wasn't bad," Richard said thoughtfully. "Not bad at all. I wonder why they didn't ask for a second *kata*. Maybe they decided you're good enough that they don't have to see any more. If you get your black belt before you're 14, Jennifer, you're sleeping in the garage!"

"Or with Max," Tim added, grinning. "He has lots of room in his doghouse."

Their teasing made me feel better, but I still didn't know why my test had been cut short with no second *kata*. It occurred to me that Richard didn't really believe I had a chance for my black belt before my next birthday—he was just trying to console me after a bad test.

Sensei Larkin came toward us, and I stood up and bowed to him. "What did I do wrong, Sensei?"

"You have to work on your kicks," Sensei lectured, but there was a faint smile in his eyes. "Two of them weren't high enough. I know you can kick waist-high and harder than you did just now. But you did a very good stomp kick. If it had connected, you might have broken your opponent's knee." He opened his hand and for the first time I saw the stripe he was holding.

"Second-degree brown belt," Tim breathed. "All right, Jenny!"

"Overall, this was a very strong performance, Jennifer," Sensei continued. "Of course, every *karate-ka* can improve. But the judges were impressed. You should be very proud."

I took the stripe from Sensei Larkin. It needed to be ironed onto my belt. "Thank you, Sensei." I bowed, and so did he.

After Sensei left, Drake asked, "Now do you start working for another rank?"

Richard pretended to scowl. "One more rank test and Jenny becomes a third-degree brown. After that, she goes for her black belt. Like I said, she'll be sleeping in the garage."

"Congratulations," Drake grinned. "I guess I'm *really* going to have to watch my temper now."

I couldn't help smiling back at him, and the look in his eyes made me feel funny. I felt older and younger at the same time. At that moment I remembered that Dad wasn't there to be proud of me. I hadn't even missed him. What was wrong with me? Was I becoming so self-centered that I didn't even care about what might be wrong with Dad?

"What about stopping for burgers?" Drake asked. "Or do you have to get home?"

"We're riding the bus," I said. I'd been too nervous to eat much breakfast, but now I was hungry.

Richard pulled out the bus schedule. "We can't get home for another hour. Let's go eat first. You'd better get changed, Jen. Otherwise, you'll be in trouble and doing push-ups again."

I saw the confusion on Drake's features and explained. "If we get in trouble in class or break the rules, then Sensei gives out the punishment, and it's usually push-ups."

"Yeah," Richard added. "When Jen and I had an argument, he gave me 200 push-ups. I was going to quit, but Mom hit the roof. By the time I got back to class, I had to do 300."

"The worst I ever got was 40," I said.

"What did you do to deserve that?" Drake asked.

"I was rude about my dad." I still felt a little guilty about that. Actually, Sensei might have given me many more push-ups than 40 for disrespect. I should feel lucky.

"I'll have to make sure I don't tell my parents, or they'll have me signed up as of yesterday!" Drake said, laughing.

I got changed and we went to McDonald's for burgers. Afterward, we took the bus home. Drake and I still needed to talk, but there was no way we could talk openly with my brothers there. And we both knew it. Drake promised to call me later that night.

"I like your boyfriend," Tim told me as we walked into the house.

I shrugged. "He isn't my boyfriend, but he *is* nice." I wanted to call Bonnie right away and tell her about the day—everything from winning the new rank to Drake's being there and celebrating at McDonald's afterward. Bonnie would be thrilled, and she would also be able to make me feel better about my dad not showing up.

The basement door popped open and Dad stuck his head out. "Where have the three of you been?"

Eight

I left Richard and Tim to explain and headed for the kitchen extension to call Bonnie. I'd no sooner dialed her number than Dad came into the room.

"Jenny?" he said.

I hung up the phone before it could ring at Bonnie's. "Yes?" I said.

Dad rubbed at the whiskers on his chin. "I'm sorry, Jenny. I completely forgot that today was your rank test. I should have been there."

"That's okay," I said, trying to hide my hurt. "Sensei Larkin said that Mom told him she'd pay the bill when she came home. He let me do the test without your being there."

Dad's dark gaze showed his worry. "It's not a question of somebody being there to pay the bill," he said. "I should have been there to show my support. Richard said you did very

104

well—much better than he did on his first try. In fact, he mentioned again how it took him three tries to win the rank you got today. He seemed very proud of you."

I started to tell him not to feel so bad, but he held his hand up for silence. His shoulders slumped and he edged toward the basement door. "I wish I had been there with your brothers, rooting for you. I'm sorry I failed you." And he disappeared down the basement stairs.

The tears rose in my eyes, and it was several minutes before I could redial Bonnie's number. Her cheery voice snapped me out of my sadness.

"Guess what?" I said.

"You got your next thing in karate," Bonnie flashed. "I knew you could do it!"

"That 'thing,' as you call it, is my next rank!" I said, laughing. "*And* you know what else? Drake was there. He came to watch me, and he bought me lunch afterward. We're going running again on Monday. And he's calling me tonight!"

"Tell me more!" Bonnie squealed. "Start at the beginning!"

We must have spent 20 minutes laughing and talking. I almost forgot about Dad and how unhappy he'd seemed. "I'd better go now," I told Bonnie. "I don't want the line to be busy if Drake tries to call now instead of tonight." That was partly true, but what I really wanted was to see if Dad was okay.

We said good-bye, and I immediately headed for the basement door. It was locked, and it stayed that way for the rest of the day. I finally gave up trying it when Drake called that evening.

Richard answered the phone in the living room. "Jenny, it's for you. Why don't you take it in the kitchen so we can watch TV?" He winked at me, and I knew he'd keep Tim out of the way.

I headed for the kitchen and picked up the phone there. "Hello?"

"Hi, Jenny. This is Drake. Do you have time to talk now?"

I looked around the empty room. "Sure. I'm sorry about the day I was late. I had to try to call my mom, and then the vice principal caught me coming back on campus."

"Did he get you in trouble with your folks?" Drake asked, and I knew he cared about the answer.

"No. He just yelled at me a lot. I still would have made it to meet you if he hadn't held me up so long."

"I was a jerk," Drake admitted. "I'm sorry.

Is your dad sick or something? Tim said he wouldn't come to the test."

I glanced over my shoulder and made sure Dad wasn't around. "It's more of an 'or something,'" I replied. "I don't think he's sick. He was just having a bad day. He'll probably be there next time."

"I'll be there," Drake volunteered. "Can you still go running with me again on Monday?"

"Of course I can," I told him. "I can hardly wait till Monday."

"No reason to," Drake answered, and I could almost see his smile in my mind. "Why don't we go tomorrow?"

I nodded, but I knew he couldn't see me. "I'd love it. Where?"

We set it up for the track in the park near my house. Drake said he'd take the bus over in the afternoon. I could have walked on air when I hung up, and I decided to call Bonnie again to share my good news. Life would seem perfect if Dad would come out of the basement. I wondered how much beer he had drunk down there, and whether he'd taken the gun back outside. And then I thought about Mom.

I dialed Mom's long-distance number instead of Bonnie's. Mom usually took the Saturday night duty. I hoped she would be there. I just had to talk to her.

A man answered and rattled off his name and something else I couldn't catch. I never could understand what those military people said when they answered the phone. "Is Sergeant Conway there?" I asked.

"No. She left about two hours ago."

I wondered where Mom had gone, and decided it was probably to a movie or something. "I'll try again later. Thank you."

I hung up and called Bonnie. She was almost as excited as I was about the running date. Afterward I went to my closet and found my newest pair of sweats. They were still clean, but I decided to wash them anyway. I scooped them up and headed for the basement. The door was still locked. Well, I thought, these sweats will have to do the way they are. I looked again at the door, then turned away and went back upstairs.

* * * * *

The next day I got up early and took a long shower. I used Mom's shampoo on my hair. She wouldn't mind, and I wanted to look my best. I put on a clean pair of jeans and a T-shirt. I would change for running before meeting Drake.

Richard wasn't in the kitchen but he must have just been there. A frying pan was on one of the burners, and it was starting to smoke. I switched off the flame. I didn't know what Richard was planning to fix, so I didn't try to help. Instead, I started setting the table.

My brother usually wasn't so careless, and I wondered what he was thinking. Dad came up from the basement, and I smiled at him. "Good morning." He looked tired. "Did you go to bed last night?" I asked.

"I'm an adult, Jennifer. I'll make my own decisions." Dad rubbed at his beard stubble and looked at the frying pan. "I started to make pancakes but I couldn't find the mix."

"I'll help," I volunteered. The pancake mix turned out to be in the top cupboard behind the cereal. Dad was quiet, but other than that he seemed almost his usual self.

"Hope you're not still mad at me about your rank test," he said to me while the pancakes sizzled.

"Dad, I wasn't mad," I said as I finished setting the table. "You've been to the others and you know what they're like. Besides, you'll come when I try for my next level, won't you?"

Dad tried to smile. "You bet I will. I just forgot about the time yesterday."

"Were you working on my Christmas present?" I asked. I could tell by the look on his face that he hadn't been. I wondered why he kept drinking and hiding from us. Didn't he know how much we loved him and needed him?

Maybe not. I walked across the room and put my arms around his waist. "I love you, Daddy."

Dad held me so tight that I could barely breathe, but I smelled the beer anyway. "I love you too, honey."

* * * * *

Drake was right on time to go running. We met in the park. We didn't talk about my dad. What more was there to say? Instead, I asked about the track team, and Drake started telling me about the meets.

"Are you going to join the team?" Drake inquired.

"I don't see how," I answered. "But I wish I could. With Mom gone, I hardly have time for karate, not to mention another sport. You know how much time it took me to get ready for the rank test. I go to class three times a week and sometimes on the weekend, too. And we have tournaments."

Drake nodded. "How long have you been taking karate?"

"Three years. Sensei Larkin says I have a lot of potential, but that I need to work harder."

"Sounds like Fisher when he's yelling at me,"

Drake laughed.

I couldn't help grinning back at him. He was right about coaches and teachers, always saying you should work harder. "How is your programming class?"

"Forget that," Drake groaned. "I'm doomed to fail."

"I bought a book for you," I said shyly. "It's all about BASIC programming, and it has step-by-step instructions."

Drake stopped and caught my arm. "You did that for me when I was so nasty to you?"

I could feel my cheeks starting to heat up. "I did it before. I know how hard it is when Richard's supposed to be teaching something!"

Drake looked at me warmly. "Thank you, Jenny. That's the nicest thing anyone's ever done for me."

"You haven't seen the book yet." I couldn't help being pleased by his gratitude. "It may not be any good at all for your class."

"I'm sure it will," Drake promised.

We started to run again. It was getting easier all the time to run exactly in step with Drake, and it seemed like the most natural thing in the world not even to talk. After three more miles, we headed back to my house. While Drake got some water in the kitchen, I went upstairs to get the computer book. He was still in the kitchen when I came back down.

"Here you go," I said, handing him the book.

Drake began to flip through the pages. "This is wonderful! It has a lot of the same stuff we're doing in class. Maybe I *will* be able to pass this course after all! Thanks, Jenny."

At that point the doorbell rang, and I went to answer it. Diana stood on the front porch. What was *she* doing here? Just when I was having such a nice time with Drake!

"I came to get my books," Diana told me, looking into the house cautiously.

"I'll get them for you," I said, hesitating. Should I invite her in or not?

"I'll wait out here," Diana answered before I could ask.

"You can come in if you want."

"I'd rather not. Your dad'll probably do something weird."

That took care of any friendliness I felt. "I'll be right back." I knew it was rude, but I shut the door in her face anyway. I headed into the living room and began to collect the library books. Even if Diana was sort of right about my dad, she didn't have to be so nasty.

"Who's at the door?" Richard asked as he came in.

"Diana. She came to get her things. But she wouldn't come in the house." I found another book and put it on the stack.

Richard didn't say anything for a moment. Then he asked, "Is she the one Dad scared?"

"Yeah." I stared after him as he headed for the door. Somehow, he got Diana to come inside and wait. Then Drake came out of the kitchen.

We all wound up in the living room. With Richard and Drake there, Diana started behaving very politely. But I still felt clumsy. I kept looking for the library books and pretended not to notice that Diana sat down on the couch next to Drake.

"Jenny bought me a computer-programming book," Drake said looking at me. I felt a little better.

"I'll show it to you." I fished out the last of Diana's books and set the stack on the table. "We were about to have something to drink. Would you like a mineral water?"

"Sounds good," Drake grinned. "I don't like pop after a run."

Richard laughed. "Well, we're out of junk food anyway till Mom gets home."

"Where is she?" Diana asked.

"On Army duty in California." I led the way back to the kitchen and started fixing drinks for everybody. Suddenly, Tim came rushing in from the backyard with Max. "Tim, he's supposed to stay outside," I said quickly. "Take that dog back out and leave him there!"

"Brad and I are doing some stuff and Max keeps getting in the way." Tim headed back outside. "You guys watch him." He slammed the door.

"And what do you suppose he's up to?" Richard questioned as he sipped at his drink.

"Probably just kid stuff," Drake said. "He can't be in real trouble, can he?"

Richard and I looked at each other. Bookworms are supposed to be passive, but Tim does try out some of the stunts he reads about.

All at once I heard a rapid pop-pop-pop sound. It was almost like gunfire, but not quite. Then I recognized the sound. "Fireworks. Brad's family didn't shoot them off last July. They were keeping some in the garage." Max pushed against me and started whining.

"I'll go stop them," Richard said. He put down his drink on the table and headed across the room.

Diana sighed. "I've never had a brother, but they sure can be a hassle, can't they?"

"Tim's okay," I said, stroking the dog. "He just doesn't think, sometimes."

"He'll outgrow it," Drake promised. "*I* didn't start out perfect, either."

Drake and I both laughed at his joke, but Diana looked shocked. I guess she didn't have much of a sense of humor that day.

I saw the basement door open and hoped Dad was going to act normal. But when I saw the way he slipped into the room, I knew better. "Dad?" He stared at me as if he didn't know who I was. We heard another round of firecrackers go off.

"Under the table! Quick!" Dad shouted.

I took a step toward him but Max was in my way. "Dad, it's just Tim. He's shooting off firecrackers. Richard already went to stop him."

Dad grabbed my arm and propelled me into Diana, pushing both of us at the table. "Get under there and stay down!" He gave Drake a shove. "You too!"

Then Dad crouched down and moved to the back door, grabbing a butcher knife on the way. In another instant, he'd tiptoed out the door and was around the corner.

Nine

"HE'S nuts," Diana stated triumphantly as we crouched under the table. "I told you that the last time."

I lifted my face from where it was buried in Max's fur. "You've got your precious books. Get out!"

"What did you say?" Diana asked.

"I'm speaking perfectly plain English! Get out!" This time I yelled it and Max got scared. He growled, but he looked like he wasn't sure why.

Diana scuttled out from under the table and grabbed her books. "Are you coming, Drake? That man is crazy."

Drake didn't move. "Jenny didn't tell me to go," he replied. "I'm staying."

She was gone in a matter of seconds. "Maybe you should go, too," I suggested. I saw the concern in Drake's eyes. "Dad won't hurt

116

me but he'll be really embarrassed when he realizes what a stink he made just because of Tim."

"Are you sure?" Drake asked.

"I'm sure," I answered, trying to speak in a steady voice.

Drake nodded and scooted out from under the table. "I'll see you tomorrow at the gym, and we'll go running."

When I heard the front door close, a sob choked in my throat. I wouldn't go to the gym tomorrow or any other day. I pushed my face against Max's side again, embarrassed to come out from under the table in my own kitchen.

The back door crashed open. "I don't see why I'm in trouble. They were Brad's firecrackers."

"To your room!" Dad's tones sounded like thunder.

Tim ran, and I didn't blame him. Dad was walking after Tim, but he stopped when he saw me under the table. "Jenny, what are you doing?"

"You told me to stay here. And my friends." I didn't move. "Do you have fun thinking up ways to humiliate me?"

"Humiliate you?" Dad scowled. "I was trying to save your life. That sounded just like a sniper back in 'Nam."

117

"I told you it wasn't," I retorted. "I said it was Tim. And you made a fool of me again. Do you have to do that every time Diana's here?"

Dad looked around. "Well, where is she now? And that boy?"

"They're gone." I glared at him. "And I don't blame them. I wish I could go, too."

Dad was quiet for a second. When he spoke, his voice was strained. "The noise just reminded me of being in Vietnam. I couldn't help it."

I petted Max again and crawled out to stand up. "I wasn't there! And it's not my fault! I don't see why I have to be punished all the time. *I* didn't make you go into the Marines. I didn't make you go to war! I WASN'T THERE!"

"Jenny." Dad reached for me and I jumped away.

I ran down the hall to my room, slamming the door behind me. That wasn't good enough. The door didn't have a lock on it, so I grabbed my nightstand and pulled it across to block it. Then I got my log-cabin dollhouse, the heaviest of all of them. I boosted it on top of the nightstand. Now I was safe.

That thought didn't cheer me up at all. I threw myself on my bed and burst into tears. I cried and cried, but it didn't make me feel any better. I was furious with my father. I hated Diana! And I was humiliated that Drake had witnessed that whole terrible scene.

I must have cried for hours, until finally I fell asleep.

* * * * *

There was a thumping at my door and I opened my eyes. "What?" I croaked. My throat felt sore, and my eyes were a little swollen.

"It's school," Richard yelled. "Are you coming or not?"

"I'm never leaving this room again," I called back. "Not ever!"

"I'm telling Dad," Richard threatened.

"Go ahead," I said nastily. I heard Richard stomp away. Eventually I went to sleep again with the morning sun gleaming in through the window.

The next thing I knew, Dad was knocking on the door. "Jenny, I fixed lunch. Are you hungry?" Dad called through the door.

I didn't answer, and he twisted the knob. But my barricade held. After a minute or two, Dad went away. I didn't care, I told myself. I was never coming out of my room even if my stomach caved in from hunger.

I waited for a while and then I got up. I pushed aside the doll house and nightstand. First I went to the bathroom, and then I headed for the kitchen. The basement door was closed, and Dad wasn't around. I fixed myself a sandwich and got some fruit, too.

The I heard the back door open. I put my plate down and swung around, ready to confront Dad. But it wasn't him. It was Mom!

I couldn't believe my eyes. She shouldn't have been home for another week.

"Jenny? Honey, what are you doing home? Are you sick?" Mom dropped her suitcase on the floor and started across the room.

I ran to her and threw myself in her arms. She hugged me tight and then I knew I wasn't imagining things—she really was home. Before I could stop myself, I started to cry again.

Mom kept holding me and patting my hair like she did when I was a little kid. "It's been awful here," I choked out.

"What, Jennifer?"

"Dad flipped out and made me and Drake and Diana get under the kitchen table because Tim was shooting firecrackers in the backyard."

Mom stiffened as the shock of my news hit her. "When did Dad do this?"

"Yesterday."

"I had car trouble or I'd have been here last night." Mom let me go. "Now wash your face. I'm going to talk to your father. Where is he? In the basement?"

"Yes, ma'am."

"Good." Mom went to the basement door and tried to open it, but it was locked. "What the devil?" She pounded on the wooden panel. "Conway, get up here! On the double!"

I thought I heard footsteps, and then the door opened.

Dad stood there for a minute and I saw the surprise on his features. Then he moved toward Mom and buried his face in her shoulder. She reached her arms around him and stroked his hair as if she had another oversized child in her arms. They were still standing there as I took my lunch and went back to my room.

* * * * *

I'd finished my lunch and had read two books about karate. I was thinking about going downstairs when there was a knock on my door. It opened and Mom strolled in, holding two cans of cola. She offered me one.

I popped the top on it. "What's Dad going to say?"

"Not much." Mom sat down on my bed. "He's asleep. Do you realize there isn't any junk food in this house?"

I took a swallow of the cola. "You know how Dad is about healthy stuff for us kids."

"You're right," Mom admitted. "You've been positively deprived the last few weeks! Want to come with me to the store and buy out the potato chip rack?"

I looked at my clock. School was still in session, and that meant I wouldn't see any of the other kids. "What about Dad? He has bad dreams. If he has a nightmare while we're gone . . ."

"Honey, your dad will be fine."

"No, I won't." Dad stood in the doorway of my room. He was wearing his jeans and a clean shirt. And wonder of wonders, he'd shaved. "I woke up, and you weren't there."

Mom got to her feet. "Don't be silly, Rick. I'll always be there." She put an arm around him. "When Richard gets home, I'll give him the keys to my car. *He* can go buy out the junk food section."

"I won't have that garbage in my house," Dad protested, but he didn't sound like he meant it.

"Want to bet?" Mom laughed, and for the first time in what seemed like ages, our household started to feel right again. Mom was home where she belonged.

Tiny, slim, and sporting all that red-gold hair, she doesn't look much like a mom, especially when she wears jeans and one of Dad's sloppy shirts. The only times she gets really dressed up are when she and Dad are going out and when she has army duty. Of course, she usually has her makeup on and she fusses with her hair, too, not that it does much good in holding the flyaway mass in place.

I really didn't feel like staying in my room, so I went into the living room to watch TV. I was there when Richard got home. "Hi. Mom's here."

"I don't believe it!" Richard looked totally relieved, and I realized he'd been under as much pressure as I was. "When did she get home?"

"Lunchtime. She's with Dad. And she wants you to drive her car to the store and get some chips and other *real* food.

Richard beamed. "I can pick up Tim, too. He went to karate by himself. He figured Dad would still be furious."

"I am," Dad said from the hallway, but Mom winked at us. Then she ran over to hug Richard.

"I do want you to go to the store," Mom

said when she let Richard out of her bear hug. "And if you'd pick up Tim, that'd be great, too. Why don't you stop at the pizza joint for dinner? But I want the three of you home before nine."

Richard looked at her and then at Dad before he nodded. "Sure, Mom. Come on, Jenny."

"I'm not leaving this house," I said firmly.

"Oh, yes, you are." Mom put her hands on her hips. "Either that or you're cleaning the backyard after Max. Your dad and I want to talk without an audience. Make a decision, Jennifer."

I wasn't being offered much of a choice. "I'll go, but I don't like it."

"You don't have to like it," Mom said. "You just have to do it."

So I did it. We made it to the *dojo* in time for me to attend class. I felt even better after an hour and a half of exercise. But I still didn't feel perfect.

As soon as we entered the pizza parlor, I froze. Drake was there playing video games, and he stopped when he saw me. I had stood him up at the running track today, and I dreaded what he would say. The last time had caused such a mess. I wanted to run the other way, but I couldn't get my feet to move. What would he say this time?

Drake started toward me. I finally jerked myself into motion and ran. He caught up with me outside. I didn't speak, and finally he did.

"I shouldn't have left yesterday. I'm sorry, Jenny."

I thought I was all done crying but I felt the tears start up again. "I couldn't come today."

"I know," Drake put an arm around me. "It's okay. When you feel like running again, we will."

I thought he didn't know I was crying, but when he got out his handkerchief, I realized he did. I slumped to the curb and gave way to tears. Drake sat down beside me, his arm around me, and let me cry until there wasn't another sob left inside me.

* * * * *

"I'm not going to school." I sat in my bathrobe at the kitchen table.

Mom was making waffles. "Jennifer." Her tone held a warning.

Dad came to the table and sat down in his chair. "I won't go to the Veterans' Administration, and that's final. There's nothing wrong with me."

"Rick, we've been over this. You promised

you'd go. At least for a checkup."

"Well, maybe I will," Dad sighed. "But not today."

Mom grimaced and turned to look at us, two truants at her breakfast table. "Okay. Then we're going to do something *I* want to do. We're going to Olympia to see the Vietnam Veterans' Memorial."

Tim came wandering in. "Jenny, how come you aren't ready?"

"I'm not going."

"You went to karate yesterday but you hadn't gone to school. It's not fair."

"She'll go back to school tomorrow," Mom stated firmly. "Today, we're going to Olympia. Do you want to come with us or go to school?"

Tim considered Dad warily. "Can I really come, sir?"

"Sure," Dad said. He grabbed Tim and hugged him tight. "You ever shoot off fireworks again and I'll skin you alive! Got it?"

"Yes, sir!" Tim hugged Dad back. "But I'd rather go to school. There are some new books due in at the library. I want to be the first to see them."

We invited Richard, too, but he had an important debate team match that afternoon. It wound up that just Mom, Dad, and I would go. Olympia, the capital of Washington State, was about two hours drive from our home in Everett.

Dad took the freeway, and I listened from the backseat as he and Mom talked about her tour in California. She told stories about running the supply room and finding toilet paper and bug spray for the soldiers, and how the driver kept forgetting to pick up the top sergeant's uniform.

The way Mom talked, the tour sounded like a lot of fun. But both Dad and I knew she'd worked too hard. She'd lost weight, and there were shadows under her eyes. I could see them in spite of her makeup. But I knew better than to say anything about it. Mom prided herself on being a good soldier.

I wondered if Mom would have time to help me convince Dad that I was serious about being a Marine. I decided to discuss it with her later. Now wasn't a good time.

The war memorials were in front of the capitol building. The first one I saw was a statue with World War I soldiers and an angel. Then there was a smaller sculpture for the soldiers who had won the Medal of Honor. Mom recognized a couple of the names and told me that there were Army Reserve centers named after those heroes.

Across the lawn and down a small hill, I saw

a long, black wall. Dad and Mom were already going that way, so I followed them. There were tiny U.S. flags by the names and flowers around the base of the wall. A jagged crack ran down part of the end section. "Dad, what does that cut mean? Did the sculptor make a mistake?"

Mom was the one who answered, "No, Jennifer. That cut outlines the shape of Vietnam."

"It looks like a jagged scar," I muttered.

Dad was staring straight ahead, and I didn't think he saw the monument anymore. "In many ways, it was, honey. In many ways, it still is." Then he went up and read a couple of names engraved on the wall. I knew he was looking at the section representing the year he'd been there the first time.

"Dad, how old were you when you went there?"

Dad's voice sounded different and not quite right. "Seventeen, Jenny. But they wouldn't let me off the ship till I turned 18."

"Some birthday present," I mumbled, and thought about Richard. He'd be 17 in another four months. And what about Drake? He'd be old enough to enlist in two years. Did I want either of them to fight in a war? *No way*, I thought.

For a moment the two of them stood still, and then Dad dug into his fatigue coat pocket, pulling out one of his medals. He carefully laid it underneath a name. Then he took out another medal and put the second one by somebody else's name.

Suddenly, I realized that these weren't just names to him, that these were people. They were men and women who'd gone to war for their country and they'd died, never to come home to their families. How many of them had been only 18, just two years older than my brother? For the first time I wondered how ready I was to join the Marines. Was I willing to die for my country?

I was only 13. Would I be ready in five years to fight a war if I had to? Would my brother be ready in one year? Not Richard, I thought. In spite of being good at karate, he really doesn't like hurting people. And Drake had his own dreams. He was going to build bridges. I didn't want to see their names on a wall like this, not next year, not ever.

I went up closer to the black marble wall, and I tried to count the names. There were supposed to be over 1,000 soldiers from Washington State who'd died in Vietnam. Were they really all listed here?

"Jenny, we're going." Mom's voice broke in

on my thoughts.

"I'll be right there." I kept looking at the wall, counting the names.

"Now, Jennifer!"

I turned and started toward my parents. When I got closer, I realized that Dad was crying. I went over to his other side and put my arm around him. And the three of us went home.

Ten

I went back to school the next day. Dad had agreed to go to the V.A., although he didn't want to do it any more than I wanted to go back to school. But if he could be grown-up, so could I. Walking into history was one of the toughest things I'd ever had to do.

Mr. Brown looked at the note from my parents. "Welcome back, Jenny. Would you stay after class, please? I want to talk to you and Diana."

"Okay," I agreed, and went to my desk. Diana didn't speak to me even when Mr. Brown told us to work on our reports. I read my history text, and she worked on the outline we'd made for the report.

After class I went up to Mr. Brown's desk. "Yes, sir?" Diana was waiting, too, and she stood a little behind me.

"Diana wants another partner for the

report," Mr. Brown said to me. He leaned back in his chair and looked at both of us. "I don't do things that way. If you two want to fight, you can. But you will do that report together. Now I'm going to take a walk, and when I come back, I want this resolved." He stood up.

"But her father's nuts," Diana protested.

My temper flared instantly. "You can say whatever you want about me," I said angrily, "but don't you ever criticize my father again. He has problems dealing with what happened to him in Vietnam. That's not his fault. He isn't perfect, but he's my dad. He always will be. And nobody puts him down!"

Mr. Brown quietly closed the door after him and Diana stood glaring at me. "Well, my dad was over there, too. He didn't act like that." Suddenly, her poise cracked like an egg. "I wish he had."

"What did you say?"

Diana glowered and tried not to cry. "You heard me. He never freaked when he heard the popcorn popper or fireworks. He never made me get under the table. He kept it all inside him. I never knew he was upset till that day . . ."

"What did he do?" I took a step closer. "Did he hurt you?" All the warnings on TV about child abuse danced through my mind.

"I didn't hug him either. Is that what you do, Jenny? Do you hug your dad and tell him that you love him? I never did. I just thought my dad knew. But I guess he didn't know how much I needed him because he went out in the backyard and killed himself!" Now Diana was crying.

"No," I gasped. "No!" I'd had no idea! As I realized how terrible it must have been, I started to cry, too. And somehow I was holding Diana while we both stood there and cried for both our fathers, and maybe even for all the other dads and moms who'd been there.

Mr. Brown came back in and hurried over to us, looking dismayed. He put an arm around me and one around Diana. "I'm sorry, girls. If you really don't want to work together, you don't have to."

"We can, now," I said and mopped at my tears. "It turns out that *both* our dads were in Vietnam. We have more in common than we thought."

Mr. Brown handed us both tissues from a box on his desk. "If you ever want to talk about it, I'm here," he promised.

"Thank you, sir." One thing still puzzled me, and I looked at Diana. "Why did you want to report on Vietnam after it killed your dad?"

Diana stared at me for a moment. "Can't you understand, Jenny? I wanted to know why he did it. I had to know."

I took a deep breath. "If you still want to, we can. There's time before the report's due."

Diana got a strange, faraway look on her face. "I don't think so. Maybe next semester. Is it okay if we keep working at your house?"

"Yeah," I said. "My mom's home now and we have *real* kid food, not things that are good for us."

"That's great."

Mr. Brown was trying not to smile. "I'll see you two tomorrow. And if you decide to do the report on Vietnam, it's okay with me."

"Thanks, Mr. Brown," I said, and Diana and I headed for the door. I made up my mind that as soon as I got home, I was going to hug my dad, just for good measure.

* * * * *

Neither one of my folks was there when I first got home. I sat in the living room and pretended to watch TV. I didn't hear the car pull in, and I was startled when Mom and Dad came in the front door. Dad was grinning, but Mom had a worried expression on her face.

"I can't believe that counselor!" Mom said,

shaking her head. "She actually thought you were dangerous."

"Now, that's not exactly what she said," Dad corrected gently. "What she said was that if I became dangerous or threatened anyone, you were to leave the house."

"Well, you'll have to do a lot more than have an occasional flashback to get rid of me, Dad," I said.

Dad smiled broadly. "Does this mean I'm forgiven for last Sunday?"

"Yeah." I ran across the room and hugged him. "I love you, Daddy."

"I love you, too, Jenny."

At dinner that night, Mom told us kids more about the interview they'd had. Dad really did have a problem called combat-related post-traumatic stress disorder. It had a shorter simpler name too—delayed stress.

People with delayed stress, Mom told us, still feel the effects of terrible experiences long after the events are over. Sometimes it could even be years later. Flashbacks, nightmares, and moodiness are just some of the ways delayed stress could affect people, she explained. Many Vietnam veterans had become victims of delayed stress. And their families, she said, are victims, too.

But now that Dad and Mom realized what

was happening, they were going to get help. Dad was going to attend group sessions with other veterans where he would learn to talk about his problem and how to deal with it. And Mom planned to attend meetings with other wives of Vietnam vets.

"What about me?" I asked. "Is there a support group for kids?"

"No, Jenny," Dad answered. "Not yet. I asked the counselor about that. He said there *is* a need but that there isn't any money to address it. You're just going to have to wait, honey."

"Maybe not," I replied thoughtfully. "Mr. Brown said he'd help me and Diana. I'll ask him if we can have our own support group. I'm sure there are more veterans' kids at my school. But they just don't talk about it."

"That sounds good," Mom said. "Sometimes I think the help you can get from ordinary people who've shared your experiences is even better than the advice you get from specialists."

"Yeah, well Jenny needs all the help she can get!" Tim said, laughing.

All of a sudden, I realized how strange it felt to joke around. Strange and good at the same time. How long had it been since all of us sat down together for a meal? How long since we laughed and teased one another like this?

The next day I waited until history was over, and then I asked Mr. Brown about helping form a support group for kids. Diana joined me to help argue my case. Mr. Brown studied us thoughtfully. Then he asked me, "Why do you want me to do this, Jennifer?"

"Because I honestly think you care about us kids," I answered. "And because I respect you. It's hard to stand up to people, but you always manage."

"All right," Mr. Brown agreed. "We'll try it and see what happens. I'll have to get permission from the principal and maybe even the school board. Why don't the two of you talk to the other kids and see how many would be interested?" He paused. Then he added, "And let's expand the focus a little bit. Let's make this a group for anybody who wants to come, for whatever reason."

"Won't that make us lose our focus on Vietnam?" Diana inquired. "That's why we need help to understand our folks."

"The Vietnam War was bigger than you think," Mr. Brown responded. "Lots of kids could have had an uncle or an aunt or a cousin who fought there."

"Or even an older brother or sister," I said, remembering my visit to the Memorial in

Olympia. "And some people who join the support group might not be relatives at all, like friends of the vets and their families." I thought of Bonnie, who'd helped me get Mom home.

"Yes, even people who are friends would be okay," Diana agreed. "Come on, Jenny. Let's go. We can start asking kids now."

"This is my free period," Mr. Brown said as he picked up some papers off his desk. "I'll go talk to the principal."

I was on top of the world when I got home later that afternoon. Mom was sitting at the kitchen table, studying the want ads.

"Mom, the support group is going to work. Mr. Brown said he'd lead it." I stopped and looked around. "Where's Dad?"

"In the basement." Mom circled an ad.

"Are you looking for a job for him?"

"Nope. For me." Mom marked another ad and then eyed me. "Honey, your dad is sick. You have to accept that. And he's not going to get better all at once. He may be this way for a long time."

"I hope not," I said. "Now that you're home, don't you think he'll get better?"

"It's going to take more than just my being home," Mom said. "It's going to take all the love and patience we can muster, maybe for quite a while. But I know we'll all pull through this. Our family is going to be just fine."

* * * * *

Later that afternoon, Mom called upstairs to me. "I'm going to the mall," she said. "Want to come?"

"Sure, but what about Dad? Will he go?"

"He'll be okay. He's working on a dollhouse."

"For me?" I asked, instantly alert. "But I want a castle."

"We're going to sell this dollhouse." Mom picked up her purse. "At least, you and I are going to try. Come on."

So we went to the mall. Mom had an appointment to talk to a man who owned a crafts store. He saw the photographs that Mom had taken of my dollhouses, and he agreed to try to sell some of the new ones Dad was making. "We've had requests for this kind of fine dollhouse before," he said. "I think this item should sell very well."

To celebrate, we headed to a nearby ice-cream shop and each bought a cone. Then we window-shopped as we ate them. "I guess I was wrong, Mom," I said as we walked along. "I really did think that when you came back home, Dad would be fine. But he's still in the basement."

"Yes," Mom agreed. "But he has us to help him climb out. Jenny, I'm not a magician. I can help your dad. I can be a partner to him."

"But you can't *make* him come up out of the dark," I finished for her, understanding her point.

"Nobody can." Mom stopped in front of a print shop. "He has to do it himself." She pointed to a poster in the window. "Have you ever seen that before?"

I read the poster. It said "God, grant me the serenity to accept the things I cannot change, the courage to change the things I can, and the wisdom to know the difference."

"I'll get you a copy," Mom told me. "It may help. Sometimes, letting another person live his own life is the hardest thing in the world to do."

I studied the poster again. "Could we get one for Diana? She needs it because her dad died, and Bonnie needs one because of her parents' divorce."

"I think we can," Mom said, smiling.

And we did get three copies. I held the sack as we strolled toward the car. "Mom, do you think a person can ever understand all this if she didn't go to Vietnam?"

"I'm not sure, honey," Mom replied. "But I know one thing. I wasn't there in Vietnam, but I can be there now for your dad. And there's something else, Jennifer. Your dad may be down in the basement, but he's always there if you need him."

"He doesn't want me to join the Marines," I finally told her. "And I don't know if I want to do it anymore either."

"You've got your whole life ahead of you," Mom reflected. "There are a thousand things I haven't done yet, Jenny. Take your time and look at everything the world has to offer. You could even be President if you wanted to."

"Except I'd have to send kids to fight wars," I said slowly. "And *I* don't want to go, so how can I send someone else?"

Mom put her arm around me. "I love you, Jen. How about if you become a karate teacher?"

"Or a marathon runner?" I suggested. "Or an electrician? Or even make dollhouses like Dad?"

"Anything in the world," Mom assured me. "You could be anything."

That night I put the poster up on my bedroom wall where I would see it every morning. Then I headed for the basement. There was one big change. The basement door wasn't locked. I could actually get in. I went down the stairs. "Dad?" I yelled.

Dad pretended to scowl at me, and behind him I thought I saw the hulk of a castle. "What do you want?"

"I'm going to have a banana split," I told him, "with lots of ice cream and topping and whipped cream and cherries and nuts. Want one?"

"All those calories," Dad groaned. "How are you going to work them off?"

"I'm running with Drake tomorrow and then there's karate." I turned. "Are you coming?"

"Yeah," Dad answered. "I am. Think we can get your mom to make her special fudge sauce?"

"We can ask," I said. And together we climbed up out of the dark and into the light.

*For the children
of the American men and women
who served in the Vietnam War.
May they have the courage
to treat their parents with the
compassion and respect they deserve.*

About the Author

As a young girl, SHANNON KENNEDY'S favorite place to dream away the days was in an old cherry tree on her family's pony farm. Shannon read many books in that tree and in the hayloft of an old barn.

Today, Shannon lives with her mother on a ranch nestled in the foothills of the Cascade Mountains. The ranch keeps Shannon pretty busy during the day, so most of her writing is done at night.

Shannon started writing in high school because the books she wanted to read hadn't been written yet. Shannon likes books about girls who do things—and Shannon has done some pretty impressive things herself. She has drawn on many of those experiences for *Daddy, Please Tell Me What's Wrong*. Shannon served in the U.S. Army, where she met a lot of soldiers who fought in Vietnam. And Shannon also studies karate, although she's nowhere near a brown belt. For the karate scenes in this book, Shannon relied on a friend of hers named Jennifer. Jenny made sure that Shannon got things right! And so did Shannon's karate teacher, Sensei Vernon McCoy.

When she's not writing, Shannon enjoys taking pictures, riding horses, and having fun with her 4-H club, the Horse Country Top Hands.